A
Shiloh
Christmas

Books by Phyllis Reynolds Naylor

SHILOH BOOKS

Shiloh • Shiloh Season • Saving Shiloh

THE ALICE BOOKS

Starting with Alice • Alice in Blunderland
Lovingly Alice • The Agony of Alice
Alice in Rapture, Sort Of • Reluctantly Alice
All But Alice • Alice in April
Alice In-Between • Alice the Brave
Alice in Lace • Outrageously Alice
Achingly Alice • Alice on the Outside
The Grooming of Alice • Alice Alone
Simply Alice • Patiently Alice
Including Alice • Alice on Her Way
Alice in the Know • Dangerously Alice
Almost Alice • Intensely Alice
Alice in Charge • Incredibly Alice
Alice on Board • Now, I'll Tell You Everything

ALICE COLLECTIONS

I Like Him, He Likes Her
It's Not Like I Planned It This Way
Please Don't Be True
You and Me and the Space In Between

THE BERNIE MAGRUDER BOOKS

Bernie Magruder and the Case of the Big Stink
Bernie Magruder and the Disappearing Bodies
Bernie Magruder and the Haunted Hotel
Bernie Magruder and the Drive-thru Funeral Parlor
Bernie Magruder and the Bus Station Blowup
Bernie Magruder and the Pirate's Treasure
Bernie Magruder and the Parachute Peril
Bernie Magruder and the Bats in the Belfry

THE CAT PACK BOOKS
The Grand Escape • *The Healing of Texas Jake*
Carlotta's Kittens • *Polo's Mother*

THE YORK TRILOGY
Shadows on the Wall • *Faces in the Water* • *Footprints at the Window*

THE WITCH BOOKS
Witch's Sister • *Witch Water*
The Witch Herself • *The Witch's Eye*
Witch Weed • *The Witch Returns*

PICTURE BOOKS
King of the Playground • *The Boy with the Helium Head*
Old Sadie and the Christmas Bear • *Keeping a Christmas Secret*
Ducks Disappearing • *I Can't Take You Anywhere*
Sweet Strawberries • *Please DO Feed the Bears*

BOOKS FOR YOUNG READERS
Josie's Troubles • *How Lazy Can You Get?*
All Because I'm Older • *Maudie in the Middle*
One of the Third-Grade Thonkers • *Roxie and the Hooligans*

BOOKS FOR MIDDLE READERS
How I Came to Be a Writer
Eddie, Incorporated • *The Solomon System*
Night Cry • *Beetles, Lightly Toasted* • *The Fear Place*
Being Danny's Dog • *Danny's Desert Rats*

BOOKS FOR OLDER READERS
Walking Through the Dark • *A String of Chances*
The Dark of the Tunnel • *The Year of the Gopher* • *Ice*
Send No Blessings • *Sang Spell* • *The Keeper* • *Walker's Crossing*
Jade Green • *Blizzard's Wake* • *Cricket Man*

• The Shiloh Quartet •

A Shiloh Christmas

Phyllis Reynolds Naylor

A Caitlyn Dlouhy Book
Atheneum Books for Young Readers

atheneum NEW YORK LONDON TORONTO SYDNEY NEW DELHI

ATHENEUM BOOKS FOR YOUNG READERS

An imprint of Simon & Schuster Children's Publishing Division

1230 Avenue of the Americas, New York, New York 10020

This book is a work of fiction. Any references to historical events, real people, or real places are used fictitiously. Other names, characters, places, and events are products of the author's imagination, and any resemblance to actual events or places or persons, living or dead, is entirely coincidental.

Text copyright © 2015 by Phyllis Reynolds Naylor

Cover illustration copyright © 2015 by Mike Wimmer

All rights reserved, including the right of reproduction in whole or in part in any form.

ATHENEUM BOOKS FOR YOUNG READERS is a registered trademark of Simon & Schuster, Inc.

Atheneum logo is a trademark of Simon & Schuster, Inc.

For information about special discounts for bulk purchases, please contact Simon & Schuster Special Sales at 1-866-506-1949 or business@simonandschuster.com.

The Simon & Schuster Speakers Bureau can bring authors to your live event. For more information or to book an event, contact the Simon & Schuster Speakers Bureau at 1-866-248-3049 or visit our website at www.simonspeakers.com.

Also available in an Atheneum Books for Young Readers hardcover edition

Book design by Sonia Chaghatzbanian

The text for this book was set in Adobe Garamond Pro.

Manufactured in the United States of America

0816 OFF

First Atheneum Books for Young Readers paperback edition September 2016

2 4 6 8 10 9 7 5 3 1

The Library of Congress has cataloged the hardcover edition as follows:

Naylor, Phyllis Reynolds.

A Shiloh Christmas / Phyllis Reynolds Naylor. — First edition.

pages cm

Summary: "Marty and his best friend, Shiloh, are on another adventure. Marty learns when a secret is too dangerous to keep, and that hate can spread like fire."—Provided by publisher.

ISBN 978-1-4814-4151-3 (hc)

ISBN 978-1-4814-4154-4 (eBook)

[1. Dogs—Fiction. 2. Family life—West Virginia—Fiction. 3. Clergy—Fiction. 4. Prejudices—Fiction. 5. Christmas—Fiction. 6. West Virginia—Fiction.] I. Title.

PZ7.N24Sgc 2015

[Fic]—dc23   2014040082

ISBN 978-1-4814-4153-7 (pbk)

To the memory of Clover,
the little dog who inspired the Shiloh series

one

You know how sometimes you look back on a simple, ordinary day, and you wonder why things couldn't be like that forever? Why just loving your own dog wasn't enough?

My dog's simple, all right, and next to getting his belly scratched, Shiloh's favorite thing in the whole world is rolling around in deer poop. Guess who has to give him a bath. The girls have their bathing suits on already. Once a wet dog goes to shaking himself, anyone within ten feet ought to have an umbrella.

I put a big plastic laundry basket under the pump in our side yard and start working the handle up and down. The very second that water splashes out, I see Shiloh's tail disappear around the corner of the house.

"Here, Shiloh!" Becky calls. Only turned four last

week, and her voice don't carry even as far as the back porch.

So Dara Lynn gives it a shot. Got her head and arms through the tire swing hanging from our box elder tree. "Here, Shiloh, Shiloh, Shiloh!" she yells, as the tire turns her round and round.

But we could call that dog till the moon comes up, and he'd still make like he didn't hear. Shiloh's learned by now that the worse he stinks, the sooner he gets a bath. Ma comes out with the teakettle and pours it all into the basket to bring up the temperature of the well water.

"Pull it out there in the sun, Marty, so he won't get so cold," she says before she goes back in.

Hard to see how anyone can get cold on a hot July day like this, the dry grass crunching every step I take. But I pull the basket out farther into the yard. Now comes the hard part, and Becky knows it'll be a while, 'cause she's got a little matchbox with a paper sail, and she comes over to float it in the laundry basket while she waits.

I walk around the house to where Shiloh's hiding under the front porch steps. Have to go through this every time Shiloh gets a b-a-t-h.

"Come on, Dara Lynn, and help," I yell.

Dara Lynn works herself out of the swing and walks

around front. She's already outgrowed the bathing suit she had last summer, and it's stretched tight across her stomach.

We both know what to do. I make like I'm going to crawl under from one side of the steps, and Dara Lynn pretends she's coming in from the other. Sure enough, my beagle scampers out from between the steps and in two seconds flat, he's up on the porch looking down on us, like it's only a game.

We both lunge at him, but Shiloh's too quick. Goes racing around the front yard in his "crazy dog" act, and the minute we give chase, he's under the steps again.

Ever since I read about the brown recluse spider and told it to Dara Lynn, we neither one of us will go crawling under the porch or anywhere else like that. It's been ten minutes now of trying to get my smelly dog in that bathwater, and Ma won't let him back in the house until we do. He'll give in finally, like he always does, but Dara Lynn and me are both hot and tired of this nonsense.

"You know what this means," I say.

"Yeah," she says, sitting back on her heels. "Let's do it."

So I go in the house and come out with the vacuum sweeper, the only noise Shiloh hates worse'n motorcycles.

Don't even have to turn it on. Shiloh sees the nozzle coming toward him, and he is out between the steps, running around the house, Dara Lynn and me after him, leaving the vacuum on the grass, and the next thing happens so fast I almost miss it:

Becky's decided to cool herself off and is sitting there in the laundry basket, chubby little arms and legs hanging over the sides, and Shiloh jumps right in on top of her. Figures he might as well get it over with.

Water everywhere, and for a couple seconds Becky just blinks and wipes her eyes. Then she sees poop on her arm.

You never heard such screeching, not even if you closed the refrigerator door on your cat.

Becky's trying to get out of the laundry basket, Shiloh keeps turning around and around on top of her, and Dara Lynn is bent over double, laughing herself silly.

"I'm *poopy!*" Becky screams as Ma comes out the back door. "Get it *off* me!" And now it's on her bathing suit and in her hair.

"Marty, what in the world . . . ?" says Ma, like it's *my* fault.

But right then the laundry basket tips over and the dirty water splashes all over Dara Lynn.

"Yaaagh!" she bellows, pulling her bathing suit out

away from her body to make the poop fall off, and she's dancing up and down, hopping on one foot, then the other.

Ma sighs. "Get the hose, Marty," she says. "This is sure a waste of good water."

Ma washes Becky's hair, I wash me and the dog, and Dara Lynn scrubs herself twice just to make sure.

I hold Shiloh's muzzle with one hand as I dry him off and look into his big brown eyes. "You are a barrel of trouble, you know it?" I whisper. And when I'm sure Ma and the girls can't hear, I tell him, "Most fun I've had since school let out."

Wish now I could have held on to that fun a little longer—made it last all summer. But there's not a single person ever knows for sure what's coming next. And whenever I get to worrying about it, the "it" is usually J. T.—Judd Travers. And I'm thinkin' now that the only other time I seen Shiloh hide under the front steps was when Judd Travers tried to take him back.

One difference between a dog and a boy is, a dog never asks *why*. I got a hundred *why*s in my head. You think a dog wonders why he was born or why he's got a tail?

But if Shiloh ever did think *why* about anything,

he must have wondered why Judd treated his dogs so poorly. Why, if they meant so little to him, wouldn't he just let 'em go?

But now that I've earned Shiloh fair and square from Judd, Shiloh knows he's part of our family. Ma forgave me for hiding Shiloh up in the woods, Dad forgave Ma for not telling him about it, and I figure the whole community has *almost* forgiven Judd for the miserable man he used to be, before he rescued Shiloh in the creek and showed he had some heart. I can't never thank him enough for that. But I can't ever seem to quit worrying about how long the peace will last.

We sprawl our scrubbed bodies around the living room, playing with Tangerine, the cat I gave Dara Lynn for Christmas last year. Got a couple feathers tied to the end of a string, and you just wiggle that along the rug and this cat does a twelve-inch leap off the floor, then pounces to the left; leaps again and pounces right. . . .

Dad comes home, drops his mailbag on a chair.

"You kids makin' that cat crazy again?" he says.

"Had one crazy animal around here today, and that was enough," says Ma, nodding toward Shiloh, who's on his belly now, lazily watching the cat.

"And he got us all poopy!" says Becky.

"Well, can't have that, can we?" says Dad. Goes out

in the kitchen and draws him a big cold drink of water from the faucet. If my dad was a dog, I think he'd be either a boxer or a mastiff. Got a square face and a nose just shy of calling big.

"Saw Judd when I made a delivery at the hardware store," Dad tells Ma. "He was buyin' a metal awning to go on his trailer. Wants a place he and his dogs can sit out in the shade."

"That's a nice idea," says Ma, her knife going *chop, chop, chop* as she dices some celery there at the counter. "Maybe he can invite a few neighbors over once in a while—show a little friendliness. He's not the only one out there on Old Creek Road."

"I don't know," says Dad. "He was having an argument with the clerk. Asked if he could bring the awning back if it didn't fit, and Mr. Bowers, he tells him not if it's dented. Judd wants to take it out of the box and make sure it's not already got a dent in it."

Dad sets his glass on the table and grins. "They were still goin' at it when I left, but no shots fired," he jokes.

Problem, I guess, is that Judd's not changed enough to suit some people. Not fast enough to suit anybody, that's for sure. He don't keep his dogs chained and hungry, the way they used to be, and they like romping around that fenced-in backyard. I haven't heard any more complaints about him trying to cheat Mr. Wallace, either, and he don't swear around Ma, leastwise where she can hear it.

But he still spits on the sidewalk no matter who might step in it. Still honks the minute the light turns green if the car in front don't take off that split second. He'll sometimes walk right by a person down in Friendly or Sistersville and never say "good morning" even when they say it first. With people wanting so hard to like him once he'd saved Shiloh, wouldn't you think he'd *try* to make it easy for 'em?

"He'll never make friends if he's always looking for an argument," I say.

"Marty, people don't change all at once," Dad tells me. "You need to have a little patience with Judd. Old habits are hard to break."

"Just think on how you still forget and leave your shoes where people can trip over them," says Ma.

"And you go right on using my pencils instead of sharpening your own," pipes up Dara Lynn, all eight years of her sassiness making themselves heard.

But Becky walks over and hands me one of her animal crackers to show that somebody in the family is on my side, and I feed it to Shiloh just to pass the favor along.

It's the driest summer West Virginia's had in sixteen years, the *Tyler Star-News* says. Last spring, Middle Island Creek was so high Dara Lynn almost drowned in it. Now each day, it seems, the water level drops some more, and things get uncovered that never should have been there in the first place—a baby carriage, for one. A stove top, another.

But it's a good season for fixing up a place, and Dad's building an extra room at the side of our house. It'll be a big bedroom for him and Ma, so I can have their old one. My sisters got the bedroom I used to have. Two girls in two beds meant I got the living room couch.

Dad thinks he'll have the new room done by Christmas, and I can't wait. Then when David Howard comes over to spend the night, we'll have a door to close, and believe me, I'll have a lock on it Dara Lynn won't be able to open in a million years.

Only chance Dad has to work on it, though, is Sundays. The other six days of the week he's a mail carrier, driving the back roads in his Jeep. Starts his day up in Sistersville casing mail for over three hundred families. After he delivers that, he drives to the post office in Friendly and does the same thing there. Pulls up to each mailbox along the road, lifts the flap, and stuffs the letters inside.

Sometimes I go along to help, especially when the new catalogs come out. What I like best is when I open a flap and find that Mrs. Ellison has left him a piece of walnut cake or the Donaldsons have put in a loaf of banana bread. We eat it right there in the Jeep.

On this last Saturday of August, though, David Howard—my buddy—bikes up from Friendly after lunch, and we're setting out with my wagon along Middle Island Creek, looking for empty bottles I might get the deposit back from Wallace's store. Aluminum cans I can get a few pennies for at the junkyard. Everything I earn goes toward the bill I owe Doc Murphy for sewing up Shiloh after that old German shepherd attacked him. That was a year ago, not more'n a week after Shiloh come to me a second time, and I'd built him a little shack up in the woods where my folks couldn't see him. And that old shepherd got in—had Shiloh cornered.

Right now I figure we've found about a dollar forty cents' worth of cans and bottles, but we've also got us an August sun so hot it'd melt the candles on a birthday cake, wouldn't even have to light the match. Shiloh trots along beside us, but I won't let him go in the water.

"How much more do you owe Doc Murphy?" David asks me.

"Not sure," I say. "May be an old man by the time it's paid off. But I do yard work for him sometimes too, and he takes that off the bill."

"You sure must love that dog," David says, wiping the sleeve of his black T-shirt across his forehead. Got a picture of a dragon on it, breathing fire, which don't make him any cooler. He's not got one ounce of fat on his body. Used to be he was heavier'n me, but now every pound he's got is pure energy.

I can see the white steeple of a small church through the trees up ahead, and David says, "Hear you're getting a new preacher."

"That's right," I tell him. "Been three years since we had a preacher at all. I can hardly remember the last one. Now the church is all scrubbed up. Ma and the girls are going to service tomorrow, but I'll be helping Dad build our new addition."

I'll be interested, though, 'cause a lot of my *whys* are in the preacher's department. Like, last fall, when Dad and I were watching football on TV, a reporter asks this quarterback how come he played so well this time, and the quarterback says it's all the Lord's doing. And then, couple weeks later, another team beats 'em, and the reporter asks the guy on *this* team how he managed to make that terrific touchdown. And *this* guy just points one finger toward heaven. What I want to know is what God's got to do with football, and just whose team he's on. Makes me cross-eyed trying to figure it out.

"What's that up there?" David says.

We slog through the weeds and jump a ditch. Shiloh's nosing around something that looks to be an old wood chair somebody's thrown down the slope, got one leg broke. Something's different about this chair, though.

David grabs the back of it and sets it up, all lop-sided. It's got wooden arms, but near the end of each one, somebody's fastened a big clamp. You can open and close them like a crab's claw.

"What kind of contraption you figure this to be?" I say.

David studies it a minute. "It's for holding some-body still, is what I think," he says. "Maybe a doctor's chair for giving shots to little kids."

"Dad could fix that leg," I say.

"If they'd wanted it fixed, they wouldn't have thrown it away," says David. He studies it some more. Then he starts to grin. "Could turn it into an electric chair, you know."

David Howard has the wildest imagination of any-one I ever met. You could tell him that a man was missing when he got on the bus at Friendly, and by the time we got to school, he'd have that man's body shot twice through the head and thrown in the Ohio River. But he's got me grinning too.

"Okay," I say. "I'll take it." And we both of us carry that chair up the bank and set it in my wagon. I almost laugh out loud, thinking how I'll play electrocution with Dara Lynn—Dara Lynn in the chair, of course. Don't know what that new preacher would say about playing that, but it's something to do the next time I have to watch the girls for Ma.

Back home, though, I carry that three-legged chair to the old shed behind the chicken coop. More I think on it, I give up the idea of playing electrocution with anyone. Too old for that, for one thing. Plus, then I'd have to explain what electrocution was to Becky, and a four-year-old wouldn't understand the logic in that anymore'n I do.

Going to save it for Halloween—put an old straw man in it, with a square head, arms in the wrist clamps, wires attached to his head, and a metal bolt going clear through it: Frankenstein in the laboratory, right out there on our front porch. Halloween's a big deal in West Virginia.

———

While Ma and the girls are at church the next morning, Dad and me manage to get the roof on the new addition, and the waterproof sheets that'll cover it till we buy some shingles. Wanted to be sure we get this done before it rains, but don't look like that's about to happen anytime soon. We're pretty proud of ourselves, though— still bragging about it while we all sit down to Sunday dinner. Becky don't want to talk about roofing, though.

"What's 'trespasses'?" she asks, pushing all the gravy to one side of her plate so it's not anywhere near touching her lima beans.

"Sins," says Dara Lynn, important-like.

"What's 'sin'?" asks Becky.

"Anything that makes Jesus sad," Ma tells her.

Dad's passing the chicken platter around the table. "So how'd the preacher do? You like his preaching?" he asks Ma.

She don't answer right away. "I think it takes a new preacher time to settle in," she says at last.

I figure that's about as lukewarm an answer can get without any ice on it.

"Wouldn't hurt him to smile a little," Dara Lynn says.

"That's true," says Ma. "But he's probably nervous his first day."

"I sure wouldn't want preaching for a job," I say, and wonder if Dad can tell I've got a piece of chicken in my hand under the table, and Shiloh's sniffing it out.

"Marty, quit feedin' that dog at mealtime," Dad says. He can tell.

"Marty always feeds Shiloh at the table," Dara Lynn pipes up.

"Just butt out!" I tell her.

"Would you two stop squabbling?" says Ma.

"They're making Jesus sad," says Becky in a pitiful little voice, and suddenly all of us start laughing. When your littlest sister begins preaching at you, you know it's time to quit.

two

September starts out dry too. The corn in people's gardens looks like it's ready for Halloween. A small shower or two just leaves folks panting for more, and I have to take a bath in Dara Lynn and Becky's water to help save it. Gross.

The faucets in our house are hooked to an electric pump that brings water up from a well. Dad won't let us use the hand pump anymore till the drought's over—wastes too much when the water comes splashing out.

Two days before school begins, Judd Travers stops by in his pickup.

Shiloh can tell the sound of his truck before any of us even know it's coming. He'll be there in the shade, tongue hanging out, waiting for a breeze, and all at once his jaws snap shut and his ears lift up. His whole body tenses, eyes fixed on the lane, and it'll be five, six seconds before we hear anything. Another five before we see the front end of Judd's pickup making the turn this side the lilac bushes.

Ma's just finished a wash in the machine on our back porch. In good weather she likes to dry the clothes outside to save on our electric bill.

"Give me every piece of worn clothing you two are even *thinking* about wearing to school the first couple weeks," she tells Dara Lynn and me, "'cause I can't speak for how much water is left in the well after today."

I give her a pair of jeans and a couple T-shirts, and she's on me right away about socks and underwear, so I have to go back and look in the corner of the closet where I keep my stuff. I come out with a handful of those. Dara Lynn, of course, has a bushel basket full, and when Ma gives a little cry, Dara Lynn says, "Well, I'm *thinking* about wearing all of it."

But finally the clothes are washed, and I help Ma hang them on the line. It's Dara Lynn's job to hand them to us a piece at a time. I'd just clamped a clothespin onto a shirt when Judd Travers pulls up in the clearing.

"Hi, Judd!" Ma calls, as he opens the door and sets one leg out on the ground. "How you doing?"

17

"Makin' out okay," he says, dragging his bad leg out after the good one. "How you?"

"Doing fine."

Shiloh's on his feet now, but he don't start toward the house. Just standing there watching, his tail as still as a fence post.

Judd's got small eyes, close together on his face, and a mouth that don't seem to open as wide as it should, like the words are coming out the corners when he talks.

He makes his way around the sheet Ma's hung on the line and comes over where Dara Lynn's waiting with a sock in her hand, ready for Ma to take it. "On my way down to the store," he says. "Hear Wallace is stocking up on gallon jugs of water, and wondered if you could use some."

"Folks are putting in a supply already?" asks Ma, resting one hand on her hip, the other on the clothesline, and Dara Lynn, squatting there on the ground, sinks down into the grass and sits cross-legged. "Sure hope it don't come to that."

"Me either," says Judd, "and the price'll go up if it does. I got no well, so got no choice. But thought I'd stop by in case you wanted me to get you some."

"I appreciate it," says Ma. "But so far the well's putting out. We're careful, though." She motions toward the clothes basket. "Have to think of all the different ways I can use the wash water before I throw it out. Wish we could have saved our corn."

Judd nods. "My tomatoes are all dried up." He looks over at Becky, who's hanging on the tire swing, waiting for me to come over, give her a push. "You like tomato sandwiches, little gal?"

Becky only wrinkles up her nose, and he laughs.

"But thanks for stopping by to ask," Ma says. "We're going to hear the new preacher again tomorrow. You heard him yet?"

Judd looks down at the ground and spits sideways. "Ain't much for preachin'," he says.

"Well, you ever get the idea to go, you're welcome to sit with us."

Judd gives a halfway nod and turns toward his truck again.

"You want me to bike over and help unload the jugs when you get back?" I ask.

"Think I can handle that okay, Marty. But if you find time to come by, chase my dogs around a little, they'd like that," Judd says.

"I will," I say. I know Shiloh won't be coming with me, though. Judd starts back to his pickup and sees Shiloh standing off under the tree, just watching. For a minute he pauses, like maybe he'll go over and stroke his head, but then he heads for the truck and drives off down the lane.

Here's the thing: If you're a stranger, and you stop, pat Shiloh on the head, talk to him in a kind voice, Shiloh's tail will start wagging the next time he sees you, he's your friend. He remembers. But if you treat him mean, if all he knows from you is a kick in the ribs, a chain holding him to a tree, suppertime comes and you forget to feed him, he remembers that too. And no matter how Judd tries—even saved Shiloh's life once—I can never get Shiloh to cross that bridge over Middle Island Creek and go visit the man who used to own him. Wonder if he ever will.

With school starting on Monday, I decide to go hear the preacher. Ma believes in going to church every Sunday, while Dad's the one who reads the Bible to himself. Says he and God have some pretty good arguments while he's out working the garden or driving his mail route.

Saturday night Ma lays out a clean shirt for me and washes Dara Lynn's hair. My sister hates to have her hair washed, even for church. We're supposed to be saving water, not using it, she says, and when that don't work, she bellows, "If God wanted me to wash my hair, he'd have sent some rain." Ma's got her head all soaped up under the kitchen faucet, and Dara Lynn's holding a towel over her face, screeching that there's soap in her eyes.

"Dara Lynn, if a little soap in your eye is your only misery, you got a fine life ahead of you," Ma says. "Now hold still."

Sunday's a steamy day for dressing up—hotter than it was the day before—but Dad's already outside, working on the new addition. I got to put on a fresh shirt and a tie.

Ties are on my *why* list. Wonder what kind of man it was who hated himself enough to design a noose around his neck. David Howard says you wear a tie just to hide the buttons on your shirt. Seems to me if that's the case, you want something pretty, you could just put bright blue buttons on every shirt so that a blue tie wasn't necessary.

At church, the parking lot's packed! Don't hold more'n twenty cars, and there's some parked along the road, too. But we file inside the little white building— CHURCH OF THE EVERLASTING LIFE, it says over the door—and find a space for the four of us in one of the pews. Not many there Becky's age, but she wanted to come anyway. Likes putting on her Sunday dress and socks.

I see the preacher—Pastor Dawes is his name—up on the platform. He's a tall man with deep creases on either side the mouth. Wears those glasses without any rims, and his hair is thin over the top of his head. Has on a brown suit and brown tie, and I suppose brown socks and shoes too, but I can't see those. He sits solemn-like as Mrs. Maxwell plays the piano, and more folks come in to find seats.

What I like most about church is the singing. We got a deacon, Brother Hatch, forty pounds more going sideways than the preacher, and he's the one leading the singing. Got the voice to do it too—as deep as a well— and he even smiles as he sings.

"Brothers and sisters," he says, "turn to page one hundred thirty-eight and sing it like you mean it!" One thirty-eight is my favorite hymn—got a rhythm that almost needs some clapping: "A Little Talk with Jesus" is what it's called.

Mrs. Maxwell plays a few notes, Brother Hatch leads off, and we all come in at the right places:

"Let us . . . ," he sings.

And the rest of us sing out:

"Have a little talk with Jesus . . ."

Brother Hatch sings:

"And we'll . . ."

"Tell him all about our troubles . . ."

"He will . . ."

"Hear our faintest cry . . ."

"And he will . . ."

"Answer by and by," we warble.

There's six or seven verses like this, and Becky swings her legs back and forth while we sing. Mrs. Maxwell slows it at the end, so we're all of us singing together, and our voices go up and down on that last note: "A . . . little . . . talk . . . with . . . Jesus . . . makes . . . it . . . riiiiigghht."

"That's just what I like to hear, brothers and sisters," Brother Hatch says, his cheeks pink from the effort of directing us. "Isn't that just the finest song?"

Everyone else seems to think so too, and I hear a few "Hallelujahs," but no telling what Pastor Dawes thinks, because those creases around his mouth sure ain't from smiling.

Becky sits all serious during Scripture reading, and then Pastor Dawes begins the sermon. I figure he's going to be loud, but he starts out soft and gentle as a breeze, and breezes are part of what he wants to preach about.

"Friends," he says, "I want to talk to you today about signs. Not stop signs. Not store signs. But signs that just might be God's way of talking to us. 'Why doesn't God talk to us the way he talked to folks back in the Old Testament?' people ask me sometimes. And my answer is that maybe he does, and we're just not listening."

So far Becky's paying attention. So's Dara Lynn, though she's got her fingers spread out on her knees, admiring the pink and purple polish on her nails.

"If you know your Bible stories," he continues, and this time his eyes seek out the children in every row, "you know how God parted the Red Sea so the Israelites could cross out of Egypt, and he closed it again on the Egyptians' chariots and men. You know how he sent the flood to cover the whole earth, all except Noah and his ark, to show how disappointed he was with his people. He made a bush to burn, a volcano to erupt, a whirlwind to take his beloved prophet Elijah to heaven, and the earth to open up and swallow those who had displeased him."

Then he reads part of a chapter from Deuteronomy about how if you obey God, he'll send rain for your corn and grass for your cattle, but if you don't, he'll "'Shut up the heavens . . . and you'll perish quickly off the good land the Lord gives you. . . .'"

I don't know how much of that Bible reading Becky understands, but she still hasn't reached for Ma's pocketbook, where Ma keeps some little slide puzzles, the kind you push squares around to make a picture. Dara Lynn sits like a statue beside me. The rest of the sermon is on the drought, and how come God sent it.

Finally Brother Hatch leads us in "What a Friend We Have in Jesus," and we're in the car again.

The sun is even hotter going home than it was coming. The girls buckle up in the backseat, and I turn down the sun visor on my side. Wish we had air-conditioning in our car like the Howards do.

Mom's a mile or two down the road when Becky says, "I don't like him."

"Pastor Dawes?" asks Ma.

"God," says Becky.

There's a gasp from Dara Lynn, and I turn halfway round in my seat. I never heard nobody in our family say that. Becky's lips are like a line in a cement sidewalk, and she's staring straight ahead.

"Why's that, sweetheart?" asks Ma, but I can guess.

"He does bad things," says Becky.

"Only if *you're* bad. *Really* bad," says Dara Lynn, the expert. "What I don't get is, if God knows everything, don't he already know we need rain? Why do we have to keep telling him?"

I'll say this for Dara Lynn, she's not afraid to ask questions.

"Maybe he forgets," says Becky.

I don't even try to get into that conversation, but Dara Lynn has a point.

"I think it's to remind us that we shouldn't take him for granted," says Ma. "Doesn't want us to go day after day just thinking the earth is always going to stay beautiful, and we don't have to take care of it."

"*I* take care of it!" says Becky. "I water my tomato plant!" And then, in a smaller voice, "Will the earth ever open up and swallow *me*?"

"No, Becky," I tell her, even though I don't know more'n anyone else. The thing is, I just can't believe in a God who would do that, so I guess Pastor Dawes'll be after me next.

Wonder if my friends ever think about stuff like this. I asked David Howard once what did he think happened to us after we die, and he said he hopes we get reborn as somebody else. I say, "Who do you want to be reborn as?" And he says, "Methuselah, 'cause then I'd get to live nine hundred sixty-nine years more."

three

'BOUT THE TIME THE FIRST TREES TURN COLOR, YOU'LL hear school buses grinding up the hills and along the back roads of Tyler County. Up until this year, me and Dara Lynn rode the same bus. But now that middle grades have classes at Tyler Consolidated High and I'm going into seventh, I got to be out at the bus stop at 6:55 in the morning. Dara Lynn gets a half hour more sleep.

The bus comes, I give Shiloh one last hug, and the doors swing open. First thing I see when I climb aboard is feet. Feet with shoes on 'em big as rowboats. And when I'm staring down that aisle at the knees and arms and shoulders to go with 'em, I figure that any one of those high school boys could pick me up in one hand and have me for lunch. Even the girls are big.

Driver must know what I'm thinking, 'cause he smiles at me and says, "Go on back. They don't bite."

Fact is, they're so busy talking and hooting and laughing at their own jokes they hardly pay me any mind at all. There's a few more of us middle schoolers scattered here and there, but I find an empty seat to save for David Howard, and the bus moves on.

Looking at all the different houses we pass, I'm thinking that our little two-bedroom house is about as small as they come, even though my dad gets a decent salary. But nobody could guess the number of years he paid for Grandma Preston's nursing care before she died, and he don't go around telling about the money he lent Ma's brother when Uncle Bill's house got washed away in a flood—no insurance, neither—money we'll never see again and he knows it.

But once we get that new addition, our house'll be that much bigger—a right nice-looking house.

Bus is heading down the winding road toward Little and stops to pick up a girl I've never seen before. She's by herself, and the driver reminds her she's left her sweater on the bench. She goes back down the steps to get it, her cheeks bright as holly berries from embarrassment.

I'm going to have to tell her this seat's saved, but

she don't even look my way when she passes. I even had a smile ready, but she don't want it. Okay by me.

Bus stops for David Howard and some other kids in Friendly. "Heeeerrrre's Da-vid!" he says, spreading his arms wide as he gets on the bus, and even the high school boys laugh. He slides onto the seat beside me. "How'd I do?" he says.

I make a buzzer sound like he's bounced off the show, and he elbows me in the side.

"Man, all I wanted to do this morning was sleep," he says.

"Me too," I tell him. "And Dara Lynn's cat was crawling around all over me before Dad even comes to wake me up. I'm going to be *so* glad when I have a room of my own."

"You said it. I'll be your first sleepover, and we will *party!*" says David.

Partying with David Howard at my place means exploring the fields outside after dark. That's what he likes to do, 'cause he don't have all the land down here in Friendly like we've got up in Shiloh. (I like to think we named our community after my dog, not the other way around.)

"You know, we have to find the middle school

entrance when we get to Tyler," I say. "I think the high school has its own wing. Their own hallways and everything. Even their own gym."

"Well, I hope I never get mixed up and wander into it. I don't want to be overhauled by any of these guys," David says, speaking for both of us.

Bus makes the turn, and we're riding along the Ohio River toward Sistersville. I've seen some of those houses in Sistersville, passed down from great-granddaddies. Three stories, some of 'em, with those little towers on top.

When the bus pulls up to Tyler Consolidated, the high school kids troop off to the new wing, and the principal's there to welcome new middle school students and tell us where to go.

David and I have different homerooms, and don't see each other again till English. We're both of us in that class, with a new teacher, Mr. Kelly.

So far, my teachers have all been nice, but this man walks in wearing a dark-purple shirt with a black tie. I'm thinking, *Who gives this guy fashion advice, a funeral director?* He don't even look at the class—just opens a black notebook and starts talking.

"My name is James Kelly, and you will address me as Mr. Kelly. I do not accept excuses for assignments turned in late; I do not tolerate talking in class; no gum, no food of any kind; and if you are absent more than twice, it will cost you points off your grade. Any questions?"

And then, don't even give us time to raise our hands if we dared, he adds, "And those rules apply to boys only."

There's a gasp like we're all suckin' air out of the same big straw. Can't believe this. And once again, without any time for us to protest, he says, "My mistake. Girls only."

This time the girls turn and stare at each other, and then Mr. Kelly starts to smile. "You didn't believe all that, did you?" he says.

And finally we all grin and say, naw, we knew him to be joking, though we didn't, and I decide right then I'm going to like the guy in the purple shirt.

He tells us that this is his first day of teaching at Tyler Consolidated, and he wants us to know that not only did he come in the wrong entrance himself, but he was looking for the teachers' lounge and walked into biology by mistake. "Nobody there but a frog," he says, and we laugh out loud this time.

Mr. Kelly goes on to say that we're going to be studying nonfiction for the first half of seventh grade, and we'll start with biographies, then move on to auto-biographies. One of our assignments—won't be due till the end of the semester—is to write two five-hundred-word essays. First one will be about an important person in our own lives. Second will be a biography of a class-mate, and we'll draw names to see who it will be. Maybe we don't think we've lived long enough to have anything to say, but he's going to show us that we know ourselves better than we thought.

At some point he remembers to call the roll, and when he says, "Rachel Dawes?" I look around and see the new girl answer. The preacher's daughter? She sees me looking at her and stares right back, not a trace of a smile. Must be a rule against it in that family.

Rest of the week goes okay; I like some classes better than others. David Howard invites me to stay over at his place Friday night, so Ma lets me put some clean under-wear and a toothbrush in my backpack, and I get off the bus with him down in Friendly.

I don't guess anyone really feels as easy in another person's house as he does in his own, but I like being at David's just the same. It's sure quieter when you don't have sisters. David don't even have brothers.

"How's the new addition coming, Marty?" his dad asks as he spears one of the small red potatoes on his plate and pops it in his mouth. Got his shirtsleeves rolled up to the elbows—just came home from work. Big lock of sandy hair falls over his forehead, same color as David's. Cheeks are dotted with tiny pits that make him look rugged, like he's climbed mountains or something. Far as I know he's worked for the *Tyler Star-News* a long time.

"Well, we got the frame up and the roof on, but no windows," I say. "Dad wanted to get the roof on before it rains."

"No telling how long that will be," says David's mom. She and Ma have the same blue eyes, but Mrs. Howard wears her hair down to her shoulders, and Ma keeps hers tied back with a rubber band. "Does your mother have a garden? I tried cherry tomatoes this year, but they're not doing very well. Everything needs more rain."

"Our garden dried up fast," I tell her. "Preacher told everyone to pray for rain, but I don't see no sign of it yet."

"I don't see any sign of it either," she says, looking toward the window, and the way David grins, I know I should have said *any* instead of *no*.

I'm trying to get a chance to eat my baked ziti, I think that's what they call it—good, too—but then Mr. Howard says, "What's Judd Travers up to these days?"

and I see David grin some more, 'cause he knows I'm trying to eat.

"Seems to be doing all right. Works part-time at Whelan's Garage," I tell him, studying the hot macaroni at the end of my fork. And when David's dad begins again, I hurry it to my mouth and swallow it down.

"A woman called the newspaper a couple days ago to say that a man who looked like Judd Travers ran off the road and left tire tracks through her flower garden before he sped off again," Mr. Howard tells us. "Said it was almost dark, so she didn't get the license number, but it was a blue pickup with only one brake light working."

I'd managed to get two bites chewed and swallowed in time to say, "Judd's pickup is green."

"The sheriff evidently told her the same thing, but she says it was too dark for her to tell exactly."

"If it was that dark, how did she know it was Judd Travers?" asks David.

"She just said she was pretty sure, that's all. Wanted me to do a news story about it."

"That's ridiculous," says David's mom. "What did you tell her, Steve?"

Mr. Howard sprinkles more cheese on top of his ziti and says, "I told her there was such a thing as a slow news day, but we weren't *that* slow, and she hung up on me."

We all laugh.

The Howards live in this two-story house with four bedrooms, one of them for Mr. Howard's computer and nobody in another. The bed just sits in it waiting for someone to visit.

David's room is full of maps and books and puzzles. There's a map on the wall he got from the Tyler County Highway Department, showing every road and river in the whole county—Sellers Road, Cow House Run, Dancers Lane. We take a blue pencil and trace every single back road and creek we've explored so far.

We play this game—take this plastic robot apart and see how fast we can get it back together—and then we watch TV for a while and listen to a band David likes called Dust and Falling Objects.

When David stays overnight at my house, we spend most of our time outside, playing on the tire swing, or exploring down around the old gristmill by the bridge. But we have to spread our sleeping bags out on the living room floor, and we don't have a minute's peace till the girls have gone to bed. Even then, Ma and Dad are still up in the kitchen—hear everything we say.

At David's, though, we sleep on bunk beds, and he always lets me have the top, even though that's where he sleeps when I'm not there. More than anything, I want a room of my own. I think it was when I had to give up my bedroom when I was nine that I began to fight with Dara Lynn. Who wouldn't, being kicked out of his own bed?

We've already taken our showers—they have city water, so they don't have to worry about a well running dry—but David jokes that he can smell my feet, so I hang one leg over the edge of the bunk so he can get a really good whiff. Then he tattoos a word with his finger on my bare sole, see if I can guess what word it is, and when we tire of that, we wait to see who falls asleep first.

David says, "You know what? Dad's writing a story for the newspaper about the oldest residents in Tyler County, and he interviewed a man who knew Judd Travers's dad."

"Yeah?" I say. "What'd he know about him?"

"Says he kept to himself, same as Judd, and was as mean as a junkyard dog," David tells me. "Every one of his kids ran off as soon as they had the chance. All except Judd. He was the youngest, I guess."

"Why'd they run off?" I ask.

"This man said Travers beat and cursed his kids. Told

Dad he was about the most hated man around. Whole place was a dump. Old cars and tires and rusty lawn mowers so you could hardly see the ground. Nobody wanted to live next to that, and there wasn't a single person who liked him."

Including Judd, I'm thinking.

David's getting sleepy now, I can tell. Beginning to talk slower.

"Dad won't put any of this . . . in his story, of course. And then their place burned down . . . and finally Judd got a trailer . . . of . . . his own. . . ." His voice trails off, and he's breathing deep.

How come Judd stayed? I wonder. Why was he left to take the beatings and cursing all by himself?

Just another *why* to add to my list, I guess. But if all a kid remembers is a dad telling him what a worthless, no-account boy he is, don't he grow up thinking everyone else looks at him the same way? And wouldn't it make him angry . . . and sad and scared and about every other kind of hurtful feeling there could be?

There's a whole lot about Judd Travers I don't know.

four

I'D STARTED HELPING OUT AT JOHN COLLINS ANIMAL Clinic last summer, 'cause I love animals and I want to be a veterinarian someday. Takes a ton of money to be a vet, I know—once you get through college, there's even more college. But if that can't happen, I'd like to be a veterinarian's assistant. This takes training too, but I can learn a lot just being a volunteer sometimes on Saturday mornings.

Dad drives me there on his way to work. Dr. Collins's clinic is attached to his house, and I'm early, so I just sit out on the steps, till he comes over and unlocks the door.

"Didn't think you'd be around much once school began," Dr. Collins says, big old smile on his face. He is one tall man—six foot four. Big head. Big ears. Big hands.

"I'll come whenever I can," I tell him. He did a good job treating a skin disease Shiloh had last June and I like him a lot.

"Well, I sure won't say no to that," Dr. Collins says. "You know what to do, so I'll go back and finish my coffee. Be with you in a while."

I pull on the gray cotton "kennel suit"—shirt and pants like the scrubs a surgeon wears. These have JCAC embroidered on the pocket—John Collins Animal Clinic. First thing I do is open the door to the dog run, let out the dogs that are spending the weekend here while their owners are away. The two setters, the spaniel, and the retriever go lickety-split along the fence, jumping around on each other and yipping, so glad to be out and stretch their legs a little. While they're tumbling around out there, I change the towels at the bottom of their kennels and refill their water bowls.

The spaniel comes in once and looks up at me, waiting for breakfast. "Not yet," I tell him. "Go finish the conversation with your buddies."

Then I concentrate on the patients. Talk to 'em real gentle. Dr. Collins hangs a little sign on the cage of any animal likely to bite, and I don't mess with those. Every animal has his name on a card above the latch.

"How you doin' today, General?" I say to a bulldog

who had a leg amputated. He'll go home today if there's no infection, I expect. I give him a good rub behind the ears, then lift him carefully and pull out the blanket beneath him, put in a clean one and change his water.

"Oh no, not you again," I say when I see the striped tabby hissing at me, cage around the corner. Been in a couple times before, after a fight. "You don't never change, do you? How you expect to have any friends, you're so crabby?" And I remember the scratch he left on my arm last time he was in.

I pass him by and go on to the little kitten, got some kind of stomach sickness, mewing pitifully. Pen's a mess. "Hello there," I say, and pick her up, cradle her in my hands. Mews like a little squeak toy, and I rub the side of her face with one finger. Make a little bed for her in a box while I clean up her pen.

"Good work, Marty," Dr. Collins says when he comes in. Tells me that Chris, his assistant, won't be in until eleven today. "Could you assist me in surgery?" he asks, and I am at that sink scrubbing up so fast you wouldn't believe.

What we've got, though, is a turtle—a large terrapin, actually, a land turtle. Dr. Collins says a neighbor brought it in early that morning—found it alongside the road with a cracked shell.

I'll bet this happens a lot—people find things and bring them in. Dr. Collins always does what he can, even though the turtle's sure not going to pay any bill. He turns the terrapin upside down to check it more closely—make sure there aren't internal injuries—and I help hold it.

"Probably hit by a car, that's my guess," Dr. Collins says. "Turtles can't breathe when they're upside down, so we don't want to keep him this way very long."

I didn't know that, but I just nod, and Dr. Collins shows me how to tell male from female. We got a he-turtle here. The crack's not so thin and fine we can push it back together and brace it, but not so wide that it'll take fiberglass filler and epoxy to fill it up.

"I think I'm just going to clean it out real well so it doesn't get infected, wrap it in sterile gauze, and let it heal," he says. "We'll keep this fella around awhile and check on him. You could clean out that terrarium back there in the corner, and we'll make him comfortable."

From the time I come in this morning to the time I leave, we have this turtle to mend, a new puppy for shots, a cat to keep for a couple days while her owner goes to a wedding, and a dog with a broken leg. When Chris comes in later—he and Dr. Collins are busy in the surgical room—I get to answer the phone. This is where the kind of soft, lazy language we use at home don't—I mean, doesn't—work. I know that if I'm going to be a veterinarian someday with a good job, I got to use good grammar, and I better start practicing now.

Dad comes, picks me up at twelve thirty. We find a Wendy's and pick up a few burgers, then eat them in the Jeep while we start delivering the rest of the mail. Dr. Collins is always glad to have me, but I think Dad likes to have me along too. He can deliver the mail a lot faster with somebody helping, and I like to think I'm good company. He pulls up to each mailbox along the road, I reach out, open the flap, stuff the mail inside, and we're off again, hardly even come to a full stop.

There are some roads I've never been on at all way up in the hills. New houses being built some places, old houses that should have been torn down in others; a new little restaurant on one corner, another shop going out of business—my dad knows 'em all. Signs along the way, TURKEY SHOOT, EVERY SUNDAY, 11 TO 3, says one. JESUS SAVES AND HEALS, reads another. And then there's WHERE WILL YOU SPEND ETERNITY? HEAVEN OR HELL?

I was thinking of starting a conversation about that last one, but if Dad says there's a real hell, I don't want to ruin my day.

Mostly, I want to have more happy times with him to make up for lying last year when I was hiding Shiloh up in the woods. That was back when he belonged to Judd Travers, and I'd promised that dog he'd be safe. Wonder sometimes if it's still on Dad's mind.

Wasn't what I'd *done*, exactly—tried to protect Shiloh from Judd so he couldn't be mistreated anymore—but that I'd kept it secret from him and Ma, and worse yet, lied about it. Lying is one of the worst things you can do in my family.

The thing is, the first time I tried to keep Shiloh away from Judd, I was honest about it—told Dad how Judd treated his dogs back then, but he made me hand Shiloh over anyway, all trembling in my arms. Guess there's a *legal* right thing to do, and a *heart* right, and anybody got a heart, I don't know how he could give that shaking, whimpering dog back to a man who kicked him in the side with his boot the minute we let Shiloh out of the car.

But that was last fall. Shiloh's mine now, Judd's changed—treats his dogs a whole lot better—I'm not lying about anything, everything out in the open. But sometimes, like, at dinner, if I don't eat all my meat, Dad'll say, "Not saving that for some other dog, are you?" the way I used to do. Or if I spend some time up in the far meadow, he might say, "You haven't got something else hid up there, do you?" It's all said as a joke, but I just wonder sometimes if he totally trusts me.

How do you ever explain loving a dog so much I done what I did? Shiloh came to *me* to help him when he first run away. Followed *me* home. Looked at *me* with those big trusting eyes, like *Please help me!* Guess you have to experience it yourself to feel it. But it made me sick in my stomach to give him back to Judd Travers. And I was the happiest person in the entire world when Judd finally said he'd let me keep Shiloh if I'd work for him for forty hours, and I did. He worked me harder than I'd ever worked in my life, but I got me a dog.

Now there's a blue sky up above, a breeze coming in the car window, and Dad's got the radio on, listening to a ball game. I open Mrs. Ellison's mailbox and there's a paper plate with a half-dozen chocolate-chip cookies on it. And they're still a little warm. She must have put them out in her mailbox only a minute before we pulled up.

That makes Dad smile, and we both of us wolf those cookies down and wave at the window, can't see whether she is there or not.

"You think you could help me on the house tomorrow?" Dad asks. "Be nice if I could get the siding on while the weather's dry. There'll be a lot of work to do on the inside, but I'll save that for cold or rainy weather."

"Sure, I'll help!" I say, like he's just offered me a malted milk to go with the cookies. But I mean it, too. All I want for Christmas is that room to be done so I can have the other bedroom. Already know what's going up on my wall—a poster of the best basketball player for the West Virginia Mountaineers; a photo of David and me crashing bumper cars at the county fair last summer, and about a dozen pictures of Shiloh.

If Dad and Ma's concerned about lying, they ought to pay more attention to Dara Lynn. First off, she argues the point.

"It don't say 'don't lie' in the Bible," she tells Dad at the dinner table that night. She's talking about her new friend Ruthie, the preacher's younger daughter, who rides the school bus with her every day. Dara Lynn's in third grade, Ruthie's in second. "I looked up the Ten Commandments, and it's not there."

"'Bearing false witness' is the same thing, so stop it," says Dad.

"Dara Lynn, you'd argue the sun didn't rise, just to

be arguing," Ma tells her, reaching over to shove Becky's cup of milk back a little farther from the edge of the table.

What brought the discussion on this time is that Ruthie, according to Dara Lynn, claims her daddy don't let nobody touch his Bible when it's open. Can never set anything on top of it, and never, ever set it on the floor. Dara Lynn gets going good and next thing you know she's telling us that if you ever *do* touch his Bible when it's open, you got to walk three times around it saying the Lord's Prayer. She's almost got David Howard beat when it comes to exaggeration. We got to divide everything she tells us by half—half true, half story. And don't none of us believe the part about Ruthie having to walk three times around the Bible saying the Lord's Prayer.

"Either you or Ruthie's got an imagination as big as Nebraska," Dad says to Dara Lynn. "And I don't think her mama would like her telling stories about her daddy every day on the school bus, 'cause we've been hearing a lot of them lately."

Ma told me once that Dara Lynn acts like she does—first-class pest and storyteller—is because she's the middle child in the family. Hasn't got the privileges of the oldest or the advantages of being youngest, and the only way she can figure to get attention is by acting out.

Can't say how many times I've made the vow to be kinder to Dara Lynn. Even promised Jesus once I'd give up quarreling with my sister for Lent. Maybe once I get me a room of my own, we'll make peace again.

five

I DIDN'T NEVER HAVE TO BRING UP THAT QUESTION about hell, because my sisters did it for me.

All Sunday morning, Dad and I work on that new addition. Ma takes the girls to church, while I'm all sweaty clear down to my underwear. Wouldn't care if the sky opened and drenched me good.

I hold up big slabs of plywood while Dad nails 'em in place. We got the frames for the windows ready, but there's a whole lot of work ahead. I stick by Dad every minute, though. Hand him tools, bring him a Pepsi, pick up any nails he drops, hold the boards while he saws . . .

Even though the drought's still on, Dad lets me use the outside pump for a couple seconds to cool down and clean up before Ma and the girls get home. I stick my whole head under—hold my mouth open and gulp the cold water while Dad works the pump handle. Then I pump for him a second or two.

We sit down to Sunday dinner—Ma had a ham in the oven—and we dig in. All but Becky.

"What's the matter?" Dad asks her, as he shovels in the scalloped potatoes.

Becky just turns her fork over and over, but I see her bottom lip tremble.

"She's worried about hell," says Dara Lynn.

We're not allowed to say that word unless we're talking about religion, which I guess we are.

"Hell?" says Dad. "Is that what the pastor was preaching today?"

"Everlasting torment," says Dara Lynn, the drama queen, and there's something bright and snappy about her eyes. She lowers her voice and imitates the preacher: "It's real, brothers and sisters. You reject God, God rejects you. Think of eternal fire, eternal pain. . . ."

"Dara Lynn," says Ma in her stern voice.

Becky suddenly bursts into tears and Ma says, "Oh, sweetheart, come here. . . ." And Becky slides down off her chair and buries her head in Ma's lap.

Ma gives Dara Lynn a look to hush her up, then glances over at Dad. "I miss Pastor Evans," she says.

"Why did he leave?" I ask, only vaguely remembering him. I weren't that much older than Dara Lynn when he left.

"He retired," says Ma. "But he was so wise."

"I don't want to burn up," Becky whimpers.

"You're not going to burn up, sweetheart," says Dad.

"The way Pastor Dawes told it, the drought's all our fault, and he made it sound like half of us were heading straight to hell," says Dara Lynn.

"Would you *stop*?" says Ma.

But I want to get in my two cents before we change the subject. "Here's what I don't understand," I say. "How are we supposed to forgive our enemies if God can't forgive his? I wouldn't want even my worst enemy to burn."

"Good point," says Dad.

"Pastor Evans only talked about God's love," says Ma. "You left his sermons wanting to be a kinder, better person."

"All Pastor Dawes talks about is sin," says Dara Lynn. "I don't know how Ruthie and her sister can stand him."

"Well, he's not your daddy, so don't worry about it," Dad tells her, and then, to Ma, "Maybe we should think about leaving Becky home on Sundays."

But Becky raises up so fast her head bumps the table.

Hell don't seem to bother her as much as being left behind; she hates that worse than anything. "No! I want to go," she says.

"Maybe he'll be preaching about something else next Sunday," says Ma. "We'll see."

I do my job of shoveling out the floor of the chicken coop. Then I ride over to Judd Travers's place late that afternoon. Shiloh sees me get on my bike, he jumps up, ready to run along. But when I turn toward the bridge, he stops and watches while I cross. And when I reach the other side, he lopes back to the house.

'Bout a half mile more, I pull up to Judd's yard. It don't look as bad as people say his dad's place looked, but Judd's not too good about taking things to the junk-yard either. There's still the old Chevy he had before he bought his pickup—car hasn't run for a couple years—a shed with a broken door, old tires. But I try not to judge people by their housekeeping.

Judd's sitting on the step to his trailer with a boot in his hand, putting a new lace in it. He sees me coming through the trees and grins.

"Well, look who showed up," he says. "Come to see me or my dogs?"

"Both," I tell him, grinning back, and I get off my

bike. Already I can hear his two dogs yipping for me out back, jumping against the fence.

"You better go play with 'em, and then I'll give 'em some supper," says Judd, picking up the second boot and poking a new lace in that.

I go round to the gate and ease in careful so the dogs don't get out. They leap up against me, nipping at each other in their excitement. Dara Lynn's not the only one acts a little nuts just to get some attention.

I pick up two sticks, throw them both at the same time so each of the dogs has something to fetch, and once they come running back, I play at trying to grab the sticks in their mouths. They run circles around me, while I chase them. Keep at it till I'm as sweaty as I was this morning helping Dad.

The new metal awning is up over the back stoop and I sit in the shade, catching my breath. The dogs come nuzzling up to me, wanting to be stroked and petted. The spotted coon dog even rolls over on his back a bit and lets me rub his belly, and the white one—a terrier mix—sits and pants for a while, then cocks his head to one side so I can scratch behind his ear, then cocks his head the other way. Judd had 'em chained up for so long they got to acting fierce just to protect themselves, but now that we put a fence around the yard and they can run, they've settled down some.

After a while Judd comes out with a bag of dry food and pours some in each of the dogs' bowls. I'm glad to see he puts a good amount in each one, not starvation rations like it used to be, and got their water dishes full too. All Judd knew of taking care of a living creature was how his dad had cared for him, but he's learning different.

We sit on that back stoop together watching the dogs push their bowls around with their muzzles until they've finished. Finally they lay down on the ground next to us, nudging our legs from time to time in case we feel like chasing 'em around the yard some more.

"How long you had this place, Judd?" I ask.

"Don't know how many years exactly. Used to belong to my pa—had a house and trailer on it. Lost 'em both in a fire, and he died the next week of a heart attack. My ma died the year before."

"Wow," I say, and scratch the terrier behind his ears. "That's a lot to happen all so close together. How old were you then?"

"Fifteen . . . sixteen . . . thereabouts," he says.

"So how'd the fire start?" I ask.

"Well . . . I was supposed to be burning some trash, but I was working on an old rowboat at the same time, trying to fix it up. Not paying good enough attention to the fire, and let it get away from me. My fault, but I didn't mean it to happen. Not that I hadn't imagined doing my dad that way a couple of times."

For a few seconds Judd just sits, slowly shaking his head back and forth. "He was the meanest cuss on the face of this earth, and he probably thought the same of me," he says.

It's sure different now, sitting here talking like this, from when Judd used to run me off, I ever got near his place. Couldn't tell back then if he was acting mean like his dogs, or if the dogs were copying him. Now the both of us sit here in the shade, looking out over the piece of yard as the sun's ready to set.

"Saw your ma in the Jeep this morning. Going to church with the girls, I suppose?" Judd says.

"Yeah." I'm watching the big ball of orange get swallowed up, bit by bit, by the woods around Judd's property, and when there's not even a sliver of sun left, the whole of the land stands out clear just before dusk sets in. "Preacher got Becky all scared about hell."

Judd grunts.

"Do you believe in hell, Judd?" I ask.

He don't answer for a while. Then he leans forward and rests his arms on his knees. Spits. "If there's a hell," he says, "I think it's what people make for themselves while they're living. Don't have to die to find that out."

That's about the wisest thing I ever heard coming out of Judd's mouth. Everything coming from Pastor Dawes, it seems, does a good job of stirring folks up. But maybe that's what a preacher's supposed to do, I don't know.

By October, it rains only once for about fifteen minutes, a warm Saturday afternoon. The second that sky clouds up, Ma has us three kids running outside with pots and buckets to catch what water we can. And when the rain begins in earnest, Ma and me and the girls all give a loud holler, and we stand right out there in the yard, faces up to the sky, just drinking it in.

Ma's reaching up with her arms, whirling herself slowly around and around like a dancer, her hair all wet down to her shoulders. I just plain lie down in the grass and let the rain pepper my whole body.

Shiloh don't like it much—runs up on the back porch—but when he sees Dara Lynn and Becky whooping it up, stomping in every little place the water's collecting, mud squishing up between their bare toes, he comes back out and runs around too. Comes over and tries to nudge me to get up. Just what we need—a wet dog smell in the house—but we don't care.

But then Ma makes Dara Lynn and Becky and me strip down to our underwear and soap up. Now if that isn't the most embarrassingly pitiful thing we ever done.

"Marty, the only one to see you besides us is God," Ma says, but I step behind the shed anyways. The girls are already squealin' about bein' outside in their underpants. We shampoo our hair while we're at it, but then the rain quits and I don't know if I got all the soap out or not. Ma checks the rain barrel under the downspout, and it's got only an inch of water in it. Still, there's a quarter inch in the pots and pans, and we'll save every little bit.

At school on Monday, I'm not the only one looks scruffy. Easy to tell who has city water and which of us depends on a well, tryin' hard to preserve it.

In English class, we draw names to see who we're going to write a biography about. I wish I could get David's and he could get mine. We'd write some really crazy things about each other. I know the one name I *don't* want to get, and when I reach in the box that Mr. Kelly passes round and pull out a slip of paper, that's exactly the name I get: Rachel Dawes.

I complain to David at lunchtime.

"She rides our bus and hasn't said one single solitary word to me since school started," I say.

"You ever said one single solitary word to her?" he asks.

"No, because I've never not once seen her smile."

"Maybe she's got bad teeth," says David.

"You even try to get near her here at school, she turns away."

"Go to her house, then!" David says. "Some people are a lot more friendly at home than they are at school. She probably just doesn't want a boy talking to her."

If she didn't want a boy talking to her at school, she probably don't want him coming by at home neither. Still, it was an assignment. *Someone* had to do it.

I put it off for a whole week. Adam Frisk drew my name, and he's already started writing about me. What I really want to do is start work on a straw man to sit in that Frankenstein chair, get him all fixed up for Halloween. Finally I tell myself I can't do that till I've interviewed Rachel and get enough for five hundred words. So on Friday after school, I look up the Dawes on our church address list and head out on my bike. I find the road where they live, make the turn, and start looking for their name on the mailboxes.

Finally, around a bend, there it is—an old two-story farmhouse, appears to be—field on both sides of it, a stand of trees on the northwest border to shield it from wind in the winter. No porch, just a small stoop, and every blind in every window is pulled exactly halfway down. Bet I could measure with a yardstick, and they'd all be exactly the same.

I been rehearsing what I'm going to say when she opens the door: *Hi, Rachel. I drew your name in English class and . . .* No. Never said one word to her up until now, so I got to start out with something more polite. *Hi, Rachel. Sorry I didn't get around to this before, but . . .*

No. That makes me look weak. Even saw her a couple times in church on Sunday and never said hi then, and neither did she.

Nobody comes at my first knock. Maybe it wasn't loud enough. So I bang real hard. And suddenly the door opens and there's the preacher looking down at me, his glasses on the end of his nose. He's got a pen in one hand, a sheet of paper in the other, and I can tell by his face he don't remember me from church—haven't been there enough, I guess.

"Yes?" he says.

"Is . . . Rachel home?" I bleat out. Sound like a sheep.

"Why do you want to see her?" he says.

"Uh . . . I come to interview her for school," I tell him.

"Why is that?" the preacher asks, and I can tell right off he don't want any boys talking to his daughter.

Why is what? I wonder, and I shrug. "To write about her for English," I say, and then I see that Rachel don't tell him much about school.

"I'm afraid Rachel's busy now. Excuse me," the preacher says, and closes the door. Softly. But in my face.

six

RIDING TO SCHOOL ON MONDAY, I NOTICE SIGNS POP-ping up on people's lawns—red and blue, red and white, some of them red, white, and blue. Must be another election coming up, I figure. I don't pay much mind to elections unless it's national; then, if we elect a new president and vice president, I got two more names to memorize for history.

This time it's a local election, Ma says, and one of the things people will be voting for is whether the county should invest in new, up-to-date science books. If you read some of the signs, though, you'd think God was on the ballot. One sign says THE BIBLE'S NEVER OUT OF DATE. VOTE NO! And sure enough, five days later, there's a billboard down on Route 2 saying IT'S RIGHT TO WANT THE BEST FOR OUR CHILDREN! VOTE YES ON QUESTION 4.

And then, coming home from school, going the other way, I see a sign along the sidewalk, A VOTE FOR GRIDLEY IS A VOTE FOR GOD.

Sure would like to know if God takes sides. Grandma Slater, Ma's mom, when she was alive, stayed out of politics completely and put it all in God's hands. On judgment day, she told us, God divides the sheep from the goats, that's all we should be worrying about. But that got me to thinking that if all the people in the world were lined up to be judged, it was going to be a mighty long time before lunch. Guess I was just hungry.

Dad strained his back working on the new addition, so this Sunday he takes a break and comes to church with us. Says it's time he met the preacher, anyway.

Find out they've started a little Sunday school in the basement for children under seven, so I figure it wasn't just Becky got upset over Pastor Dawes's sermon the week before. Becky don't want to go to it, though—wants to sit with us, but since they're giving out Jesus sticker books, she finally goes downstairs. So it's Dara Lynn sitting between our dad and mama, and she has the smile of a saint on her face.

To the preacher's credit, he don't preach politics neither. First off, he's new around here, so he don't know

Gridley or any of the other people on the ballot. But he sure knows about sin, and this morning he's on his favorite topic. I tell you, that man has 150 ways you can sin without even thinkin' about it.

"Make no mistake," he says, leaning forward, hands holding tight to both sides of the pulpit, "God knows all your excuses. He knows how you can slide right into sin while telling yourself you're only human. . . ."

Then he looks square down at our faces, and his eyes travel from one row to the next. "How many of us ever looked at a neighbor's new car and wished it was ours? How many of us spend some time with the sick or dying and make sure our neighbors hear about it? How many of us have let our eyes wander over to someone else's paper for an answer on a test?"

Now his voice gets louder: "You may love God like you should, but do you *fear* him like you should? Do you imagine for one moment he can't read the most private thoughts that ever passed through your head?

"Brothers and sisters, we may already be worshipping the wrong god, the god of *money*"—and he brings his fist down hard on the pulpit, *BANG!*—"the god of *power*"—another bang—"the god of *self-conceit*"—*BANG!*

Dara Lynn likes all the noise, I can tell. I see her slide

a small smile up toward Dad, but he don't take his eyes off the preacher.

When he ends his sermon, Pastor Dawes says we've got to be the Lord's soldiers. We've got to be his army, fighting sin wherever we see it—in ourselves, our families, our neighbors, and our community. . . .

We sing "Stand Up, Stand Up for Jesus," Mrs. Maxwell playing the piano, and the service is over.

Ma's already made friends with the preacher's wife, and as people make their way up the aisle, she and Mrs. Dawes are talking about the weather. Everyone's praying for rain again. That one short rain we had was the only one we've had in months.

Mrs. Dawes is a thin woman, and probably a whole foot shorter than her husband. A whole lot quieter, too; not pretty, not plain—tired-looking, is how I'd describe her. And the little purple flowers on her gray dress don't do a whole lot to brighten her up.

"Judith, this is my husband, Ray," Ma tells her. Mrs. Dawes puts out her hand, and Dad shakes it.

"Good to meet you," he says. "Your family beginning to feel settled here?"

"Oh, yes. We're used to moving," Mrs. Dawes says. "Always hard on the girls, though," and she makes this little gesture toward Rachel, who's standing four feet away, head turned toward the windows. Dara Lynn and Ruthie are already whispering little secrets to each other as they inch up the aisle with the rest of us.

"Our younger daughters ride the bus together," Ma says. "We hear a lot about your Ruthie."

"Well"—Mrs. Dawes moves two steps forward, stops again—"she's a regular little chatterbox. . . ."

I'm thinking this would be a good time to tell Rachel I got her name for a biography, but she's workin' so hard to keep her distance that I sort of wimp out. Not due till Christmas anyhow.

In the hallway, Becky comes scrambling up the stairs from below, waving her sticker book, and Ma grabs her hand so she won't push her way out through the door.

The preacher's there, shaking hands with everyone, and when it's Dad's turn, he says, "I'm Ray Preston, Pastor Dawes. Haven't had a chance yet to welcome you to our community."

The pastor searches his face to see if he's someone he remembers—decides no. "Thank you," he says, and there's at least a half-inch smile on his face. "I believe I've met your wife."

"Yes, you have. I can't come every Sunday because

I need to finish a building project before winter sets in, but I hope to hear more of your sermons."

I think the preacher's going to nod, but instead I hear him say, "Well, where your priorities are, there will your heart be also."

And Dad says, "True. And right now my priorities are with my family. Nice to meet you." And I follow him out.

It's a quiet Sunday afternoon without Dad sawing and hammering out there on the new addition. He's in the recliner with a pillow behind his back, and I watch a football game with him. We usually root for the Pittsburgh Steelers, but today we're cheering the Giants.

I sit on the floor with Shiloh. I'm propped against the sofa, and he lies with his head on his paws, eyes closed, but I'll see his ears twitch if there's a loud blast of noise from the TV. It's like he's sleeping and listening both at the same time.

He'll get up and wander off now and then if he hears a sound in the kitchen like maybe somebody's opening a can of meatballs and didn't invite him. But one time, when he don't come back, I go get a snack for myself, and then I notice that Dara Lynn and Becky's bedroom door is closed. That's an almost sure 100 percent that they're into mischief.

I go stand with my ear against the door, and all I get are giggles.

I knock, and they scream and Shiloh yips.

"Don't come in!" Becky yells, but if my dog is in there, I'm going.

I open the door and see them trying to push Shiloh into the closet. At least I think it's Shiloh, because he's got a red kerchief around his neck, one of Becky's white T-shirts over his chest and front paws, and a fringed skirt around his belly, with a pair of pink underwear pulled up high on his hind legs.

"What are you doing?" I say. "Get that stuff off my dog!"

"It's his Halloween costume!" says Dara Lynn. "He's cute!"

"He's a cowgirl!" says Becky, and then she bolts out the door before I can catch her, Shiloh at her heels. Next thing she's in the living room by Dad's chair, tapping his arm to see Shiloh.

But there's a penalty being announced at the football game, and the referee is adjusting his microphone.

"Shhhh," Dad says to Becky, his eyes never leaving the screen. "I want to hear this." He pats his legs for Becky to climb into his lap, but Shiloh thinks it's for him and jumps instead.

Us three kids are standing there, our mouths half-open, as Dad feels the fringe of the cowgirl skirt on his lap, and still watching the TV, he gives Shiloh's rump a little pat.

Then Shiloh wags his tail, flip-flop, right against Dad's hand, and suddenly Dad jerks back and stares down at the dog.

"Becky!" he yells, and I'm laughing harder than I can remember, right along with my sisters. I come out here to bawl 'em out, and all I can do is double over. Ma comes in from the other room, and she's laughing too.

"Two girls in this family is enough!" Dad says, grinning now. "Would you let that dog be a dog, please, and let me finish watchin' this game?"

The next week the preacher's wife calls and asks Ma if Ruthie could stay at our house awhile after school on Wednesday. She's got to take Rachel to the eye doctor, and there's like to be a long wait at his office. Mrs. Dawes would be glad to return the favor anytime Ma would like to leave Dara Lynn with them.

"Would they keep her for a year?" I say when Mom tells us at the dinner table, and she gives me her look.

Wednesday I come home from school and here's this skinny-legged girl—skinnier than Dara Lynn, even—

sitting on top of the tire swing, her legs crossed beneath her, hands holding tight to the rope, and Dara Lynn on a stepladder, holding her back. Dara Lynn lets her go, and Ruthie sails out across the yard screechin' her lungs out, but when she sails back again, she bumps into Dara Lynn, knockin' her off the stepladder, herself off the tire, and then Becky jumps down off the porch and piles on top of them, all three of them laughing and shrieking. Never heard such high-pitched sounds in all my life. I go in the house and shut the door.

Ma smiles. "It's not so bad with the door closed," she says.

But later they come inside, and Dara Lynn and Ruthie are on the phone, tryin' to convince Mrs. Dawes to let Ruthie stay for dinner. Finally she agrees, as long as Dara Lynn will come to dinner someday at their house.

When Dad gets home, though, Ruthie gets quiet, and at the dinner table, she eats with her eyes down. She's got a long, thin face, like her pa, and her light-brown hair hangs in wisps around her ears. Dad asks her a few polite questions, and she answers like every word she uses costs her a nickel.

So Becky takes over. Chews for a while, her eyes on Ruthie, and then she up and says, "Why do you have to march three times around the Bible?"

This time Ruthie's head comes up and she stares back. I see Dara Lynn squirm.

"What?" says Ruthie.

"Why do you have to march three times around the Bible if you touch it?" Becky asks.

Ruthie's eyebrows scrunch up, trying to puzzle it out. "We can't touch it when it's open, but we don't have to march. . . ."

And Dara Lynn, trying hard to change the subject, says, "But you had to put your feet in ice water."

Now Ma and Dad have stopped eating.

"That was only once, for something else," Ruthie says, and drops her eyes again.

Dad steps in. "Well, we're glad you could join us for dinner, Ruthie. I already peeked in the kitchen and see some apple dumplings out there."

When the dusty black car pulls up around seven, the preacher gets out and stands by the car, and Dad walks out with Ruthie. I watch from the door.

Preacher and Dad shake hands.

"Nice to see you again, Pastor," Dad says. "We enjoyed having Ruthie join us for dinner."

"I trust she behaved herself," the preacher says.

"Absolutely. A pleasure to have her at our table."

"Bringing them up in the way of the Lord is the hardest work I ever did in my life. Scripture promises that if we do, they will not depart from it, but it's a struggle, isn't it?" Preacher says. And without waiting for an answer, he slides into the driver's seat and starts the car.

If Rachel is supposed to be wearing glasses at school, she don't want anyone to know it. Mr. Kelly is talking about autobiographies now, and he hands out a list he wants us to read—choose two, he says—and I see Rachel squinting at the list. In math, though, we've still got blackboards, and we're supposed to copy down some problems from the board. I see her dig a pair of glasses out of her bag, put them on, and take them off the minute she's through. Sees me looking at her and gives me this scowl as if to say, *So what?* I see that look a lot. Ma calls people like that "prickly." Like they're ready to be offended whatever you do or say.

Every few weeks I ride over to Doc Murphy's, see if there's any job I can do for him that would take a little off the bill I owe him for fixing up Shiloh. This particular day he asks can I clean out one of the cupboards in his kitchen—got sort of sticky since his wife passed away, and it's not something a man pays much attention to.

He's right about that, 'cause the syrup bottle and the ketchup and the salad dressing have all left circles on the wood shelf. I set to work taking everything out and wiping the shelves clean.

Doc Murphy sits at the table, slicing up an apple and some cheese for us to eat when I'm through. Today we're talking about the drought. Well, water, anyway.

"Did you know," asks Doc, "that since the world began, not a single drop of water has been added to the earth, or a single drop taken away?"

No, I tell him, I didn't know that, and I give the ketchup bottle a good swipe around the bottom.

"What it means is we can't afford to waste it, because the more people there are on the planet, the less each person gets," he tells me.

"So it's not like there's a big reservoir in the sky God could let loose if he wanted?" I say.

"There's whatever has been sucked up by evaporation from the oceans, and at some point it will come down again as rain," says Doc.

"You don't think the drought's because God's mad at us?" I ask.

"I believe there are cycles to nature, and not all of them are to our liking," he answers.

He goes on cutting up apple, I go on cleaning shelves.

I wonder if I'm pestering him with these kinds of questions. After a while I say, "Guess I've got a lot of *whys* in my head."

"So do I," says Doc. "And the longer I'm a doctor, the longer I work with people, the more *whys* I get."

At the animal clinic the next Saturday, Chris is busy tending to a cat got all torn up by a raccoon, so Dr. Collins asks me to come in and help while he puts a dog to sleep.

People still want to call it that, nobody brave enough to call death by its real name. When people die, it's somebody "passed." Here it's "put to sleep."

The lady who brought Ollie in says she's had him since he was eight weeks old, and now he's been alive for thirteen years, sick for two. Dr. Collins tells me Ollie's heart's failing, kidneys are failing, and he suspects he's got a tumor somewhere, giving him pain.

Miss Bowen can't hardly stand being in the room when Ollie gets the needle, but can't stand not being there neither, so she wants all the loving hands on her pet we can provide, and Dr. Collins asks can I come in and stroke the dog till its over.

Miss Bowen has her hands on Ollie's head, her face against his muzzle. I'm stroking Ollie's flank.

"Ready?" Dr. Collins asks, real gentle.

"Oh, Ollie, I love you so," the lady sobs, and I got a lump in my own throat.

Dr. Collins gives the needle, and Ollie don't even jerk or flinch. His breathing stops, and a few seconds later Miss Bowen raises up and looks at him, and his eyes look just like glass marbles, not moving at all.

I hope I don't have to assist in any more going-to-sleep sessions, but I'll have to if I get to be a vet. Every time a dog comes in hurting, I think of Shiloh.

Even though I'm going home at noon this time instead of helping Dad deliver mail, he stops at Wallace's store in Friendly so I can buy me a PayDay candy bar—the way I treat myself for helping out at the clinic. Split it with Dad. Be nice if I could ever get a real part-time job at the clinic—get paid with money, not candy.

Ma had a headache this morning, so after Dad drops me off at home, she lies down for a nap and I keep the girls quiet out on the porch making a straw man. We've got us an old pillowcase, an old shirt and overalls of Dad's, and a raggedy pair of work gloves, and we're cramming them full of straw. We'll have that man sitting out here on the porch come Halloween. Dad says we can have the bale of straw he got for the chicken house to use for stuffing, and after Halloween's over, we'll give it back to the chickens.

Shiloh's lying beside me, glad for a bit of sunshine, and Tangerine's jumping at every twitch of his tail, trying to catch it.

I found a perfect box for the head, and Becky's stuffing the arms. Dara Lynn took the job of patiently pushing crushed straw into each finger of the work gloves.

"See how real they look if I don't make 'em too stiff?" she says, holding up one glove. "We can bend 'em a little at the joints."

Becky lifts her head and scrunches up her nose. "What's that?" she asks, and sniffs.

I'm sniffing at about the same time. "Somebody must be burning leaves," I tell her. "Against the law when it's so dry."

"I smell it too," says Dara Lynn.

I put down the box and look out across Middle Island Creek, at the woods far off on Old Creek Road. I see a cloud of gray smoke rising up over the tops of the trees. Then I go out in the yard and climb on top the shed.

It's getting windier, and I can't tell if the smoke is all in one place or moving along. All in one place, it's probably somebody's trash pit. But far down, I see this yellow-orange color, and it's moving. Dancing.

I jump down and yell, "Go inside and wake Ma. Tell her there's a fire! It's coming down Old Creek Road. And don't you move from here 'less Ma goes with you."

And leaving Shiloh and the girls behind, I leap on my bike, go racing down the lane, and thunder across the planks of the bridge.

seven

ALL I CAN THINK OF IS JUDD'S DOGS, PENNED UP IN HIS backyard. Judd's been working six days a week now at Whelan's. Don't get off till five. Can already see them in my head, smelling the danger, yelping and throwing themselves against the fence, trying to get out.

I pedal like mad, all the while hoping that maybe a neighbor's already opened the gate—the one neighbor close enough to see, anyway. But deep down I'm thinkin' that anybody who looks out and sees smoke and flames coming their way is probably going to think first of their own pets and babies, and how much of their things they can throw in the car in two minutes.

Quarter of a mile away and I can hear the barking— a frenzy of yips and howls, and I'm scared to death the flames have already got there. Heart's beating so hard it can't go no faster. Neither can I. My legs ache, and I'm terrified to be heading right for the inferno, but I've already got my own strategy: once I see it's only twenty yards off, I'll drag my bike down the bank and throw myself in the creek.

A car's comin' down the road toward me and swerves to let me pass—hardly room, with trees on one side, creek on the other.

"Get out of here, boy!" a man yells out his window. "Place is on fire!"

"I will," I yell back, but keep going. So does the car. Far, far away, I hear a siren.

Reach Judd's brown-and-white trailer, and I half fall off my bike. His pickup's gone, of course. I race around the side, the dogs so terrified they almost bite at me as I'm trying to work the latch. I swing the gate open and they run like rockets.

Then I think of Shiloh. Think how someone let Judd's dogs loose once out of spite, back when the dogs was kept chained and mean, and how they went running through the neighborhood, tearing stuff up. One even bit Dara Lynn on the hand. Now that Judd's been treating his dogs better and I been playing with them some, they aren't nearly as bad as they used to be. But who knows what two dogs will do, scared half out of their minds, if they come upon a small child or a trembling little beagle.

So I'm on my bike again, going fast as my feet will pedal, and this time I can see the yellow-orange coming through the trees behind me, not as close as twenty yards, but I can hear the snap of branches falling, the hiss of the flames. Smoke is getting thicker, and I hit a rock and almost go down, but manage to keep the bike up. The dogs could be anywhere—could have crossed at the bridge or headed off into more woods farther on.

I reach the bridge myself and speed across those wood planks, thinking how the fire could eat them up, my heart beating so fast it hurts. Head up the lane toward the house, and I'm screamin', "Dara Lynn, get Shiloh and Tangerine in the house! Hurry!"

She's standing out there beside Ma and Becky, Ma turnin' this way and that, trying to make sense of what's going on—the smoke, the fire sirens, and me yelling.

"Shiloh!" I scream again. "Get him and your cat inside! Hurry!"

Dara Lynn don't bother to ask why. For once in her life she just does what I say—runs on up to the house where Shiloh's standin' at the door, tail between his legs, knowin' something awful's in the air, grabs up her cat, then opens the door and shoves them both in before she runs back down to Ma.

"Marty!" Ma calls, swinging herself around. "Where *were* you? Which way's that fire going?"

But I don't answer and she don't press me, 'cause a fire engine's coming along the road up from Little—a good big one—must be from St. Mary's, and the siren's going so loud can't hear nothing but that. I drop my bike, and all four of us go hurrying down the lane. See the truck stop at the bridge, half blocking the road so's cars can still get out, but nobody can drive over there.

Firemen jump off, unrolling the hoses, and even though this one siren stops, we can hear more in the distance. Fire trucks are coming from all directions, trying to find the best place to fight those flames.

Two firemen pull a hose onto the bridge and aim it at the glow coming at them through the trees, big spray of mist, not a thick stream of water like I'd expect. Three more men are hauling some equipment down the bank, getting ready to use a portable pump to refill the engine's tank with creek water.

"Oh no! Oh no!" Ma keeps whispering to herself over and over, one hand to her cheek, the other on Becky's head. We can't see what's behind the fire, just one big mass of gray smoke, but we know there's some houses in that woods. Some right nice ones too. Cars are coming to a stop now behind the fire truck, men won't let them cross the bridge even if they got a house over there. People get out of their cars and come down to stand by us.

"The drought's turned the whole woods to kindling," one woman says. "Do you suppose there's even enough water in the creek to fight this thing? Water level was already down two feet."

"It's all we've got," a man answers. "No hydrants up here."

A tall tree, burning, falls to the ground on the other side, and the whole sky seems to light up for a minute or two, the flames so high, sparks going everywhere, setting more dry brush on fire.

Becky pulls Ma's hand away and looks up at her. "Is that hell?" she asks in a tiny voice.

Ma swoops down and lifts her up, hugs her. "No, Becky," she says, trying to sound calm. "This is just a terrible accident that shouldn't have happened."

Dara Lynn's crawled up a crabapple tree so she can see better. The line of cars behind the fire truck is longer, more coming all the time. Then I see this dark-green pickup come barreling up over the hill. It slows down, like all the others, then swerves over onto the shoulder, front tires in the field.

Judd Travers jumps out and starts running toward the bridge.

"I got to see Judd," I tell Ma, and I'm running up the road to meet him.

By the time I get there, though, Judd's standing still, one hand to his forehead, eyes fixed on the fiery woods across the creek and the blackened land behind it. Suddenly his legs seem to give way. He squats down there in the road and buries his head on his arms.

I stoop down beside him.

"Judd, you okay?" I say.

"My dogs . . . ," he's saying, over and over.

"I let 'em loose, Judd," I tell him. "I don't know where they went, but they run off."

He jerks around. "You got 'em out?"

"Yeah, I was—"

But I don't get a chance to say any more, 'cause he's got one arm around my shoulder so hard I almost sit down on the ground.

"Thank you, Marty. Thank you," he says.

And then, almost as though he'd just thought of it, he says, "My trailer burned up, didn't it?"

"I suppose so," I say, and he just nods.

We hear another car door slam and then loud crying, and it's one of Judd's neighbors. One of the Donaldsons, I think.

"My house! My house!" the woman screams, and she

just goes on screaming and screaming, pounding her fists on the roof of her car as neighbors put their arms around her.

I'm thinking what Ma once said—that if there was ever a fire or a tornado coming, the one thing she'd grab once her children were safe would be the photo album of family pictures. And I wonder what this woman's grieving most, or if it's just all of it together.

I can't tell how wide the fire burned, but after a long while I see firemen coming through the burned-out woods from the other side. Sirens are still wailing, though, more and more trucks coming, wanting to be sure every last spark is out, and I suppose some men will be on duty all night long to see it don't flare up again. On the other side of the bridge, the black branches of burned-out trees stretch to the right and left, on and on.

Then I see Dad walking along the edge of the road way down, mailbag over his shoulder, past the line of parked cars, everybody gathering near the bridge. Figure he had to leave his Jeep, couldn't get through.

Firemen are pulling one of the hoses back to the truck.

I wave, and Dad sees me at last.

"Marty, are your ma and the girls all right?" he calls, and I nod. When he gets up to where I'm standing, he says, "I hear it took out some houses along Old Creek Road." And then he sees Judd. "Judd, I'm so sorry . . . ," he says.

Judd lets out his breath, don't say a word.

"Listen. You're going to stay with us tonight and have some supper," Dad tells him.

But Judd shakes his head. "Gotta find my dogs," he says, and starts back along the road toward his truck.

The Red Cross shows up with sandwiches and coffee for the firemen and the families who lost their homes. Five houses, along with Judd's trailer, been burned to the ground, and six or seven more been smoke damaged real bad. An announcement goes out on TV that cots will be put up in Sistersville Elementary for folks to spend the night.

Church is full up the next morning, and Dad comes too. Ma says it's times like this that bring a community together, and now we got a pastor to help us through it. She was on the phone the night before, calling to bring a dinner dish to church, to be carried down to Sistersville. The food is placed on a table near the back before it's transferred to a station wagon and driven off. So all the while I'm sitting in the pew with my family, my nose has the memory of ham and fried chicken, and I wish I'd eaten a bigger breakfast.

It's a somber service. Mrs. Maxwell plays "God Will Take Care of You," and we sing all four verses. Then Pastor Dawes goes to the pulpit.

"Our hearts are heavy this morning as we grieve with all the families affected by the fire," he says. "But despite the destruction, no one lost his life, and Lord, we thank you for that, for if your eye is on the sparrow, as the Bible says, then it surely is on us."

I hear some "Praise the Lords."

But now the preacher's restless-like; turns his body one way as he talks, then turns it the other. He leans over the pulpit and then rears back, like he can't get comfortable any which way.

"But what is God's message?" he's saying. "Brothers and sisters, the Lord has sent both a drought and a fire upon us. What will it take to turn us back to God? In the last perilous times of this earth, the Bible tells us, men will become proud, boastful, and haters of God. Children will be disobedient to their parents, unthankful, unholy. . . . "

I'm glad Becky is downstairs putting pictures of Jesus in a sticker book.

"Let us use these punishments to look into our own hearts. Have we lived up to the Lord's teachings?

Have we demanded obedience of our children? Have we preached the gospel to our neighbors?"

Pastor Dawes takes out a handkerchief folded into a four-inch square and wipes his forehead. Then he goes on quoting the Bible, but somehow I think he's leavin' a lot out: "The Bible tells us that if a neighbor acts unholy and neglects to hear the church, 'let him be unto thee as a heathen man,' lest worse things fall upon us. . . . "

What the heck does that mean? I wonder. Seems to me the preacher's saying that if us church folks aren't to blame for the drought and the fire, then somebody else is, and we got to find out who.

One thing I've decided on my own, though—I've got to tell Ma and Dad that I let Judd's dogs out. I was disobedient in going over there, because I knew they wouldn't want me anywhere near that fire. But maybe this is one way to show Dad he can trust me to tell him stuff. He'll be angry, knowing the chance I took, but he'll be glad I'm not keeping it from him neither.

Don't think it's just me; everybody seems unsettled as we're leaving the church. Some edge around the ones in the doorway who are shaking hands with the preacher and go right out to their cars. Others stay to tell him it was a thoughtful sermon, gave us something to think about.

We pass Doc Murphy, getting in his old Ford sedan.

"What did you think of the sermon?" Dad asks him.

"Well, I've heard worse, and I expect the pastor's given better," he says.

Dad has the car radio on to hear if anyone knows yet how the fire started. A reporter's talking how donations of food and clothing are being brought to Sistersville Elementary, and Dara Lynn wonders if people will still be sleeping there when she and Ruthie go to school the next day.

"I don't think so," says Dad. "Some of them are waiting for relatives to come pick them up, and some are moving in with neighbors. I'm going down this afternoon and see how I can help—take folks to the drugstore to get things they need; drive them to the bus station."

I can see right off that Dad and I aren't going to do any work on the new addition today. I was planning to tell him as soon as we got home about how I let Judd's dogs loose, but now I'm not sure.

A woman on the radio's talking about how the Lord blessed her, because the fire came right up to the edge of her lawn and stopped. Didn't even get as far as the kids' swing set, she says. But why would God save *her* house and let the others burn to the ground? I'm wondering. If I had saved Judd's brown dog and let the white one die, wouldn't that be wrong? How come it's okay if God does the exact same thing?

When we pull up to the house and get out, we see a trail of paw prints going up the porch steps and over to the window in our living room. And the glass is all smudged on the outside where an animal has been close up. Inside, Shiloh is barking up a storm.

eight

"Looks like Shiloh's buddy came by while we were gone," Ma says, opening the door to let him out. Shiloh likes to explore the woods with a black Lab that comes over from time to time—the Ellisons' dog.

But just to be sure it wasn't Judd's dogs, I follow Shiloh around to keep him safe while he does his business before I take him back inside. Dad's already at the table, and Ma takes a roast from the pot.

"C'mon, girls," Dad says. "Let's eat."

We're passing around the pole beans and turnips, and Ma says, "I don't know, Ray. Can't see how anything Pastor Dawes said this morning is helpful right now. Pastor Evans would have talked about the love this community has shown each other in the past, and how we're called on now to be as generous as we can."

Dad reaches over and cuts up Becky's meat for her. "Well, I suppose most preachers have a favorite subject they like to talk about, and Dawes sure seems to have a lot to say about sin."

"He doesn't seem like a happy man," Ma goes on, and then she stops, glancing at Dara Lynn and Becky, like she's already said too much.

"Well, Ruthie thinks he's *mean!*" says Dara Lynn.

"You shouldn't be going around repeating that," Ma tells her. "Everyone probably thinks their parents are mean from time to time."

"Bet you tell your friends *I'm* mean," Dad jokes.

Dara Lynn's got her mouth full, but she shakes her head.

"No? What about that time you were squeezin' that squeaky toy on and on and I told you to stop and you didn't?"

Dara Lynn's eyes open wide with the memory. "And you grabbed it out of my hands and threw it out the back door and we never did find it." Her face is full of delight and mischief. Anytime Ma or Dad makes a mistake, she rolls in it, like a dog rolling in something nasty.

"Actually, we did," Dad says. "*I* found it, anyway. It was out there in the tall grass, and I ran over it with the lawn mower."

Both girls gasp and stare at him, then start to giggle.

"So wasn't I mean then?" he asks.

"Yes," Dara Lynn decides. "But you never made me mix up all the food on my plate and put it in my milk and drink it."

"What?" I say.

"Dara Lynn, don't exaggerate," says Ma.

"I'm *not*! Ruthie told me. When she was in first grade, she was playing around with her food—dropping pieces of bread in her milk—and her dad said she had to mix up the leftover food on her plate and put it in her milk and drink it down for all the starving children in Africa."

"Let's not repeat things like this in front of a four-year-old," Dad says, nodding toward Becky, who's staring, mouth open.

Ma changes the subject, but after Becky slides down from her chair to go watch the cartoon channel, Ma says, "Dara Lynn, I don't mean to pry into your friends' lives, but has Ruthie ever said that her father hurt her in any way?"

"He hurts her *feelings*!" Dara Lynn says defensively. "But he don't hit her or nothing that I know of."

"Well, please tell us if he does," Ma says.

After Dara Lynn goes into the living room to watch

TV with Becky, Ma's rinsing off dishes in the sink, Dad's there with his coffee, and I figure this is as good a time as any for my confession.

"I got something I want to tell you," I say, and get it over with fast. "I let Judd's dogs loose before the fire got there."

I think I've said it clear enough, but they look like they don't understand.

"What do you mean, *before* the fire?" Dad asks.

"I mean . . . before the fire got that far," I tell him. "Just before the firemen came."

Ma grabs the back of her chair and slowly sits down, dish towel in her lap. "You went *over* there?" she asks. "That's where you were?"

"Marty!" Dad puts his coffee down so hard it thumps the table. "What in the world were you thinking?"

"I know I shouldn't have, but Judd was at work and I knew his dogs couldn't get out, and—"

"You risked your life for two dogs?" cries Ma.

And even though the three of us are trying to keep our voices down, Dara Lynn's right there in the doorway, taking it all in.

"I had my escape all worked out," I say, which wasn't entirely true. "I could see the flames way back in the trees, and I promised myself if it got up to twenty yards behind me, I'd drop my bike and roll down the bank into the creek." Telling it now, I leave out the part about trying to save my bike, too.

Dad lets out his breath and pushes away from the table, then just sits there staring at me. "You think fire's that predictable? Don't you think a spark could set the brush on fire along the creek and travel faster than you were going on your bike? Marty, you could have been trapped before you knew it!" His face looks all pulled out of shape.

I swallow.

"I could have kept this secret," I say, like maybe I'd at least get points for that. "I didn't have to tell you."

"I'm just so—so—astonished at your poor judgment!" Ma says. "I can understand how you'd want to save those dogs, but can you even imagine the grief you'd put us through if anything happened to you?"

"I just . . . just didn't think it would," I answer. "But now, I see how it might. . . ." And then I shut up and wait for my punishment.

Dad shakes his head. "I don't know what to say," he says at last.

I don't know either. Seems like every time I get in real trouble, it's over a dog.

And this time it's caused a second problem. . . . Now I'm going to worry every minute Shiloh's outside that

Judd's dogs will come by and tear into him. Don't know if they've calmed down any or are still half-crazed over the fire.

I lay low that afternoon, doing my homework for math. Still got till the end of the semester to interview Rachel and write her biography, so I put that off once again. Read the other autobiography I've chosen for English. I've already read *Bad Boy* by Walter Dean Myers, not no accident I chose that, I guess, and now I'm reading one by Gary Paulsen.

I help Dara Lynn with her spelling, trying not to do or say anything that will make things worse between me and my folks. Dad telling me that he don't know what to say is almost worse than a punishment, because it don't clear up anything at all.

He spends the afternoon in Sistersville, and when the Jeep pulls in about five o'clock, Judd's pickup is right behind it. Dad comes into the kitchen—Judd waiting there in the doorway.

"Lou, Judd got a sleeping bag from the Red Cross, and he'd like to sleep outside here for a while and see if his dogs don't come back," Dad says.

Judd shifts his feet uneasily. He looks tired—needs a shave.

"I could stay right out on the porch and be gone when you wake up in the mornings," he says. "I'll try not to be any trouble."

"Well . . . of course, Judd! But you're not sleepin' anywhere till I get some dinner in you," Ma says.

"Thank you, but I had me a big supper down there at the school," Judd says.

"Listen. We've got an old tent we've used for family camping," Dad tells him. "Why don't we set that up, and you can leave your things in there while you're at work—not have to be clearing out every morning. At least it would be someplace to stay while you're thinkin' what to do."

Judd turns that over awhile in his head. "Appreciate it. Thanks."

I feel bad that the first thought going through my head was that Ma might put me back there in the girls' bedroom and let Judd have our couch. That he's agreed to live in a tent seems to make us all happy.

I put on my jacket and follow them outside—help clear away some brush to make a level spot where we can set up the tent, no tree roots digging through the ground—and I bring Dad's hammer so he can pound in the stakes.

Ma gets together some towels and soap, a jug of

water, a flashlight, a basin . . . I don't know what all . . . and gives them to Judd for his tent. A pillow. A blanket. Dad even finds him a Coleman lantern back in our shed. There's a rickety old outhouse up in the woods, girls won't go in if you paid 'em a hundred dollars, but Judd says it'll do.

"Is Judd going to live here now?" Becky asks. She never liked him much before, and I don't know that she likes him any more now.

"Till he figures out his next step," says Ma. "He wants to be outdoors so his dogs can find him."

"Do you think they'll ever come back?" asks Dara Lynn.

"Only thing he's got left, besides his truck. Sure hope so," says Dad.

And this would be the perfect time for one of my parents to turn to me and say, *Marty, you did a brave thing, rescuing Judd's dogs, even though it was dangerous.*

But they don't.

There's no Halloween up here this year. Most times cars drive up full of children, take them from one house to another for trick-or-treats. Sometimes older kids ride up in the back of a pickup, and that's most fun of all.

But this year, with all those burned-out houses across

the creek, and the ones full of smoke on their walls, don't seem like a time for celebrating. So the Lions Club down in Sistersville puts on a Halloween party for kids four to twelve. I don't want to go—it'll just be little kids there—but Ma wants me to keep an eye on the girls. She looks in her ragbag and finds old torn shirts and ripped-out pants for our costumes. Then she stitches a couple patches on them, messes up our hair, and smudges our faces with ash from the potbellied stove in the living room.

"Look at us, Daddy!" Becky crows.

Daddy puts down his magazine. "Why've you got your good clothes on?" he asks.

"Daaaddy!" the girls cry, and he laughs.

He goes to the closet for his jacket and finds a dirty old cap of his. Puts it on my head, and I grin at myself in the mirror. If I find I'm the only one there from middle school, I can just pull the cap half down over my face.

"I'll be back at nine," Dad says when he drops us off. "If the party's not over, I'll wait."

There's a pirate man at the door to make sure kids don't sneak back out. They don't want parents dropping their children off for a party, only to find out later they went somewhere else.

I got to say, it's a pretty good party. A clown comes over pulling this great big wagon, and it's got the youngest kids in it. Becky climbs in, and the clown tells me and Dara Lynn to go have a good time with our friends.

Takes Dara Lynn about five seconds to see some girls from third grade gathered around a fortune-teller. I'm about ready to pull Dad's cap over my face when I see David Howard and Michael Sholt lined up for an eyeball contest. See Fred Niles over there too. We'd all said we weren't coming, but we did.

A zombie leans over this huge pot of intestine-looking stuff, and each contestant has ten seconds to plunge his arms in the guts, searching for eyeballs and pulling them out. We have to compete in groups of five, so we're looking around for someone else to join us.

Sarah Peters comes along, and we yell at her to come over.

"What do I have to do?" she asks, looking down into those cooked noodles.

"Stick your hands in there and look for eyeballs," Michael tells her.

"Eeeuuu!" she says, and backs away.

But Laura Herndon comes over. "I'll do it!" she says.

So we got us a bum, a vampire, an alien, a Batman, and a cowgirl. David Howard goes first.

I can see in the pot. Noodles are slippery-looking and gooey, and David pulls out a Ping-Pong ball with a black pupil in the middle, and little red veins painted on the white part. He finds two more.

"Gahhhh!" Fred says, and we laugh.

When it's my turn, I roll up the sleeves of Dad's old shirt and plunge my arms in the pot, fingers spread out, hands feeling around in every direction. Get two eyeballs . . . then four . . . and then the zombie presses the buzzer.

I don't get a prize for this contest, but David and Laura and Sarah and I are off to another one—we choose partners and see how fast we can wrap the other one up like a mummy in toilet paper.

David says he'll be the mummy, and when the whistle blows, I got my roll of paper in one hand and I'm wrapping David's head up so fast you won't believe.

"I have to breathe, dude," he says, so I leave a little slit for one eye and an open place for his nose and I'm down under his chin wrapping his neck and his left arm. Sure is a waste of toilet paper. On my third roll and then my fourth, and I don't even bother to see what the competition is doing. I get his belly and his butt, his left leg, his right. . . . Then I see I missed his right arm, and I'm up there wrapping and Dara Lynn's out there cheering, and finally the whistle blows and I done it.

We win.

Both David and me get these little pencil boxes that look like a mummy's casket from Egypt, with a painted pharaoh on the front, his arms crossed over his chest, gold on his cheeks and forehead. Cool.

Becky comes by in a little electric car driven by another clown, who toots the horn. They're headed off to the ghost bubble dance, where a ghost blows bubbles and the little kids dance around, try not to let any land on them.

The Lions Club throws a good party, I'll say that, and I'm thinking maybe it's one of the best. I'm over at the refreshment table, a chocolate doughnut in one hand, cider in the other, when Fred Niles says, "Hey, you know who started that fire?"

"Somebody started it?" says David.

"Judd Travers," says Fred, his mouth full of doughnut.

"What are you talking about?" I say. "He was at work! And his own trailer burned to the ground with all the rest."

"Just like he did to his pa's house," says Fred, as though he didn't hear nothing I said.

"How do you know that?" asks David.

"Because somebody saw him fill up a jug of gasoline at the station a few hours before that fire started," says Fred.

The doughnut in my mouth feels like dirt.

"That don't mean anything," I say.

"He did it once, he can do it twice," says Michael Sholt.

And then the witch at the door announces the party's over, telling us all good night, and winks at me with one scaly eye, like she's in on it too.

nine

Rain.

Like the sky opens and lets loose everything it's been saving for the last three months. Too late for people's gardens, though. It runs down the windshield of the school bus, the wipers going *whup . . . whup . . .* and we have to make a run for it once we get to school. I drop my notebook and have to pick it off the rain-slick driveway, my hair soaking up water like Ma's sponge.

I shake my head hard inside the door, the drops flying every which way.

"Sorry," I say to Rachel as she goes by, and this time she smiles a little. Maybe she's not so stuck-up. I realize she wasn't at the Halloween party, though. Ruthie neither.

Too bad the rain didn't come one week earlier and

put out the fire, I'm thinking as I walk to my locker. Paper says they're still investigating the cause of it— won't rule out arson yet.

So now we got another kind of fire going—the rumor traveling around that it was Judd who started the blaze, and that moves faster than flames. Fred announcing it there at the party, and again on the bus the next morning, and every kid taking hold of it and carrying it home, means that most every family up where we live and down near Friendly has heard about Judd Travers buying that jug of gasoline. I make up my mind that I'm going to ask Judd about it myself.

In English class, Mr. Kelly's talking about the way authors start their stories. Especially the story of their own selves, and he's sitting on the edge of his desk wearing jeans and the reddest shirt you ever saw, "fire-engine red" I guess you'd call it, which don't help get my mind off the fire.

But he's talking about all the different ways you can start a story about yourself:

"Tell me what you might guess about the person who wrote this," he says, and reads, "'My family is American, and has been for generations . . .'"

He waits while we think about it, and Sarah holds up her hand.

"Somebody who thinks this is really important?" she says. "Where your family is from and everything?"

He nods. "All right. Now here's another one: 'I was born in a house my father built. . . .' Thoughts?"

"Like . . . he's starting from the beginning?" I say.

"Yes. A much simpler, closer focus. But both of these autobiographies were written by presidents of the United States: Ulysses Grant wrote the first one, Richard Nixon the second. Anybody want to read the first line of an autobiography you've chosen?"

Laura reads the first line of *Anne Frank: The Diary of a Young Girl*: "'On Friday, June 12, I woke up at six o'clock and no wonder; it was my birthday.'"

"Any thoughts about the way that begins, Laura?"

"She began it not knowing what was going to happen to her family at the end."

"That's right. Of course, none of us know what will happen in our future. But what makes Anne's diary so absorbing is that most readers *do* know what happens— that her family will lose their lives to the Nazis after they've been hiding out for two years, and as we can see from the beginning, Anne used to live a very comfortable, happy life. Someone else?"

Michael Sholt reads the first line of Tony Hawk's *Hawk: Occupation: Skateboarder*: "'I felt the cold wind that blew in from the San Francisco Bay whip across the top of the vert ramp and onto the deck as I walked around waiting my turn.'"

"What's happening here, Michael?" asks Mr. Kelly.

"He's competing in the best-trick contest at the 1999 Summer X Games," says Michael.

"So he chose to jump right into the action—a very different beginning from 'I was born in a house my father built,' but both are very effective. Adam?"

A tall boy over by the window reads the first line of Jerry Spinelli's autobiography, *Knots in My Yo-Yo String*: "'Like much of my life until that sixteenth year, it was a sunny day.'"

"What word does Spinelli use to tell us that something's going to change?"

"'Until,'" says David Howard.

"And does something happen right after that, Adam?" asks Mr. Kelly.

"Yeah. His dog gets run over."

I know right then I'm not going to read that book for a while. I really like Jerry Spinelli's books, especially *Wringer*, but I'll wait to read this one until I'm feeling strong.

I would have read the first line of the book I chose,

but I forgot and left it home—Gary Paulsen's *My Life in Dog Years*. Almost everything I do has a dog connected to it somehow.

Every day, after Judd leaves work at Whelan's, he stops off at one of the other men's houses on the way home to shower and clean off all the grease, buys his dinner somewhere, then comes to our place and crawls into the tent. In between, he says, he drives around looking for his two dogs. Didn't even name 'em. And now I'll bet he wishes he had. How can you call a dog if you got nothing to call him? Soon as the weekend comes, I'm going out on my bike and look for them too.

Ma invites Judd to eat dinner with us, but he don't. She saves a little something for him anyway and puts it in an old tin milk box out on the porch. Tells Judd to check it before he goes to the tent. And tonight, there's a light rain falling, and I'm sitting out there on the porch waiting for him, Shiloh beside me.

"Why don't you eat it out here where it's dry?" I call as he closes the door of his truck and comes over to the porch. Shiloh don't get up. Just gives Judd a sniff and stays close to me.

"It's dry in the tent," Judd says, opening the lid of the milk box and taking out the little foil-wrapped package.

"Yeah, but I'll keep you company while you eat," I tell him, so he sits down, collar turned up around his neck. It's early November, but not too cold yet.

"Your ma sure does make good cornbread," he says, after he swallows a mouthful.

"I know," I answer. And then I come right out with it: "Hey, did you run out of gas the day of the fire?"

"Now where'd *that* come from?" Judd asks, studying me as he takes another bite.

"'Cause you were getting a gallon of gasoline at the Exxon, and I just wondered, did your tank go empty?"

He smiles a little. "What you doing? Spying on me?"

"No, but someone else saw you, so I was just asking," I tell him.

"Well, Sam Beringer called me to say his truck's runnin' on empty and he don't figure he's got enough to drive to a gas station—would I pick some up for him. So I drove over to the station on my lunch break and got it. But . . ." Judd shakes his head. "No use for it now. Lost his house *and* his truck in the fire."

Judd could be lying, of course. But I believe him.

"So what'd you do with the gasoline?"

"Put it in my truck, of course. Not going to throw it out."

Wonder if I should tell Judd about the rumor going

around, but decide no. I'll tell my folks, though, and after Judd says good night and goes to his tent, I do.

Dad just shakes his head. "Some folks always have to have somebody to blame," he says. "Last year they were saying it was Judd who killed that man down in Ben's Run, remember? You'd think they'd learn a little about spreading rumors. Guess Judd's got a reputation that just won't quit."

But it was only last year that the newspaper ran a story about him rescuing Shiloh, too. Wouldn't you think that would change some minds? Don't take much to ruin a reputation, I guess, but a heck of a long time to build it back up again.

County paper comes out on Thursday with pictures of all the charred burned-out houses and cars along Old Creek Road. Last week they had pictures of the flames high as the trees, and smoke rising up toward the hills. And the article says its been confirmed now—the fire started in old Mr. Weaver's kitchen, where he'd left a pot of beans cooking on the stove; he was outside checking to see if there were any more green tomatoes left on the vines. Forgot the beans. Not a single word about arson.

Grandma Preston used to say that some people

wouldn't recognize the truth if it sat at their table and ate off their plate. But I'm thinking that part of the problem is folks take Pastor Dawes's sermons to heart about looking for sin in yourself and your neighbor, 'specially your neighbor. 'Cause after Dad picks me up at Dr. Collins's clinic on Saturday, we stop at Wallace's store again, and I run in to buy a candy bar for Dad and me to eat with our bag lunch. Got the JCPenney catalogs to deliver this afternoon along with the mail. Dad's listening to a football game, so he stays in the Jeep.

Judd's there, third in line at the counter, buying a sandwich before he goes back to work at Whelan's.

"Hi, Judd," I say, and go on over to the candy rack.

"How ya' doin', Marty?" he says.

The two women ahead of him have frown lines on their foreheads as Mr. Wallace bags their groceries. One of them turns to Judd and says, "I'm surprised you'd show your face around here."

Judd's as surprised as I am.

"Why not?" he says.

"You'd best show your face in church before you go walking around the community," says the other woman, picking up her grocery sack and hugging it to her chest. "Never saw you there once."

"What church is that?" says Judd, still puzzled. Mr.

Wallace looks embarrassed, taps the woman on the arm, but she ignores him.

"The new preacher at Church of the Everlasting Life has been preaching about people like you," says the first lady. "Everyone knows you set that fire."

Judd's had enough. "Church of Everlasting Lies!" he says. He reaches around her, plops his money on the counter, and without waiting for change, barges through the door and on outside.

The women stare after him.

"Did you hear what he said?" one of them gasps.

"You accused the man unjustly," Mr. Wallace tells them. "The inspection ruled out arson."

But just like Dad says, some people don't want to hear the truth. "Everyone knows how he set his father's house on fire when he was a teenager," the shorter woman says.

"That's not true either," I put in. "It was an accident."

The women turn and stare at me. "You weren't even alive then. What a mouth on you!" the friend says.

Mr. Wallace shakes his head. "That all you want, Marty?" he says, looking at the candy bar, and takes my money. Gives me the change as the women go out the door. "It's an uphill battle for that man," he says. "Fate never did smile down on him much."

What I really got on my mind, though, are Judd's dogs.

"You see any stray dogs around here?" I ask him. "One's white, one's brown. They were runnin' loose after the fire, but nobody's seen 'em since."

"Don't believe so, Marty," he says. "There was a collie loose for a time, but the owner got him back. Whose are they?"

"Judd's," I tell him.

Mr. Wallace gives a low whistle. "Trouble just can't let that man be, can it?" he says. "I'll keep my eyes open, let you know."

All afternoon, as I ride around with Dad dropping off those catalogs, my eyes are on the countryside, looking for Judd's dogs. On Sunday I help Dad work on the new room. Then I take off on my bike, stopping every once in a while to whistle, see what happens.

A crow answers back. That's it.

Rachel finds out I drew her name, so I can't put it off any longer. As we're leaving class, I say, "Got to get together sometime so I can interview you for that biography."

She shrugs and says, "Whatever," so I guess that's an okay.

Mr. Kelly says it would be a good thing to visit each

other's houses if we can, but it's not required. Just give a bit more local color to our piece.

"Would you come with me next Saturday?" I ask David. "I think maybe she'd be more comfortable if it wasn't just her and me. I'll even bring Shiloh, make things seem more easy."

"She knows we're coming, doesn't she?" David asks.

"Not exactly," I say, and I don't tell him that all she said was "Whatever." But I'm thinking if I call first, preacher's going to say no. Don't want any boy coming to see his daughter. But if we just show up together, David and me, maybe it'll be different. And maybe Mrs. Dawes will answer the door, or even Rachel.

I skip work at the animal clinic this time, head for Rachel's house instead, Shiloh trotting along beside my bike. David rides his up from Friendly and meets me about eleven. We park our bikes against the front stoop and go up the steps together. David rings the bell—a good hard ring.

We wait and wait, but nobody comes. Nobody at the window, that we can see. David gives me a look. "*Told ya*," he says.

We go back down the steps, and I'm wondering what do we do next. Shiloh's been sniffing at the shrubbery, and now he's disappeared around the corner of the house. I give a whistle, but he don't come. I don't want him doing his business where he shouldn't, so David and me go after him.

Nice yard in back. Flower beds all dried up, of course, but got little fences around them. Know just where you're supposed to walk and where you shouldn't. A shed, couple of trees, ash cans out by the alley.

Shiloh's loping all around the edge of the yard, and I'm just about to call out to him when I hear something. Someone. Somebody crying. At first I think it's a cat, but then David nudges my arm and says, "Listen."

When it comes again, Shiloh makes a beeline for the shed. David and me look at each other. Shiloh's standing there, ears alert, eyes fixed on the narrow door.

Now a couple of sobs come from the shed. Sound like a girl—could be either Ruthie or Rachel, can't tell. There's a slide lock on the door.

"Rachel?" I call.

The crying stops right off. Silence.

"Hey, Rachel?" I say again.

And then a soft voice says, "Who's out there?"

"Me. Marty Preston. David Howard's here too. And my dog. I wanted to interview you for our assignment. Why are you in there?"

No answer.

"You want out?" says David, and without waiting any longer, he slides the bolt and opens the door.

Rachel's standing there, nose all red and runny, and all she says is, "Wait. I have to use the bathroom." And she makes a run for the house.

We stare at each other.

"What the heck . . . ?" says David.

"You suppose she and Ruthie were playing a game and Ruthie forgot she was in there?" I say, trying to figure it out.

We look around the shed. Everything in order. Garden tools on hooks, hose all coiled up, baskets of hand tools—trowels and hammers and screwdrivers . . . Rachel could probably have pounded one of those aluminum walls down if she had to. But where is everybody?

A couple minutes later, Rachel comes out the back door, and she goes straight into the shed.

"Lock the door again," she says. "Hurry!"

ten

"WHAT?" I SAY.

But there's panic in her voice. "Hurry!" she says again. "Before my dad gets back."

"He put you in here?" David asks, holding the door fast as she tries to close it.

"Please!" Rachel begs. "I'll really get in trouble if you don't."

"I just wanted to do that assignment," I tell her again.

"We'll do it at school. At lunchtime, maybe, okay? Please, just close the door and lock it."

We close the door.

"Where's your ma and Ruthie?" I call out.

"At the doctor. I'm being punished. You really need to leave," she tells us. "Lock the door."

And her voice is so panicky that we slide the bolt. But

we don't ride off. No way are we going to leave her here like this. What if there was another fire in the neighborhood and she couldn't get out? The preacher would do this to his kid?

There's no house close on either side, but we get on our bikes and take them back to the stand of trees where we can't be seen. And we sit there on a fallen tree trunk, our eyes on that shed. I got a finger around Shiloh's collar and tell him to sit.

It's ten minutes before the preacher's car shows up. We hear the car door slam. Then the front door of the house. But nobody comes out.

The anger inside me is churning around like a lunch gone bad.

"If I was in that shed, I'd be tearing the place down," I tell David, my jaws tight.

"I'd call the police when I got out," David whispers back.

"She don't even have a jacket, and it's really cold in there. Could have got one when she went in the house, but then, I guess, he'd know she'd been out."

After a few more minutes, David says, "Think *we* should tell the police?"

But just then the back door opens and the preacher comes down the steps. He walks out to the shed, his back straight, arms down at his sides. You'd think he was in the army.

"Are you ready to be obedient?" we hear him call to Rachel.

I guess she don't answer, because he says, "I'm waiting to unlock the door, Rachel."

And when she still don't answer, either his heart or his curiosity makes him open the door. Rachel pushes past him like a soldier herself— won't give him so much as a look.

He grabs at her arm. "I asked if you—"

"I hate you! I hate you!" she screams, and jerks her arm free. Then she breaks into a run, crosses the yard, and thunders up the back steps. Door slams.

Preacher stands there a long moment looking up at the house, his face a puzzlement. Then he puts one hand to his forehead and stays that way a good six, seven seconds. Looks like a man who's lost his way and can't make out the map. Then his shoulders lift in a slow kind of sigh, and he walks back to the house.

David and I spend the next couple hours riding around, asking folks if anyone's seen two stray dogs, a brown and a white one, but no one has, and finally David goes on home.

That night, after the girls are in bed, I tell Ma and Dad about Rachel in the shed. Don't want Dara Lynn hearing any of that and spreading it around school.

Ma listens with one hand over her mouth, then turns to Dad. Both of them been sitting together on the couch, feet sharing the footstool, watching the news.

"Ray, I think it's time to do something," Ma says.

Dad mutes the TV and thinks for a minute. "I don't see that we're called to do anything," he says.

"Why not? I think we should report it," says Ma.

"We report that a girl's been locked in a shed for a while as punishment, we got to report every family we know who still gives their child a spanking, or takes a switch to his legs."

"Then maybe we should!" Ma says fiercely, and Pa takes both feet off the footstool, places them firmly on the floor.

"Lou, a parent's got a right to discipline his kid," he says. "Maybe not the way we'd do it, but one will sit his child in the corner, the other puts his child in the shed. I can't go sayin' one's okay, the other's not."

"Even if he puts a child in the shed, out in the cold, and locks the door? And drives away?" Ma says. She realizes her voice is too loud and sinks back against the couch cushion.

"Marty don't know how long he was gone for sure. Don't even know if the preacher maybe parked somewhere nearby where he could keep an eye on things. You said yourself we've never seen either of those girls with cuts or bruises on them." He turns to me, still standing in the doorway. "You ever see Rachel come to school with a black eye?"

I shake my head. "But I never looked at Rachel and saw happy, either."

Dad leans forward and puts his head in his hands. "You're right about that," he says. "Never saw a member of that *family* look happy, to tell the truth. But you don't go reporting a family for not being happy."

Ma's got her arms folded across her chest, and she's tapping one elbow with her finger. "I'm going to see what I can find out from Mrs. Dawes," she says. "Judith and I are working together on the Thanksgiving dinner we're serving the families that were burned out. I'll find a chance to talk with her then."

"Where you going to have it?" Dad asks.

"I think we can squeeze everybody in that basement room at the church. A few of our other families are going to eat with them, so they won't feel so much like charity."

I know right away that one of those families will be

us, having our Thanksgiving dinner there this year to keep the Old Creek Road families company. But what I'm feeling is that everything's hanging, nothing settled: we don't know what'll happen to Rachel; the burned-out families don't know what's going to happen to them; Judd don't know if his dogs will ever come back; and I don't know when I'll get a room of my own. Don't even know how long it'll be before my folks feel good about me again. Wish I'd be punished, just so I could have it over and done with.

Sometimes I think I can handle bad news better than I can handle being unsettled, everybody just waiting. . . .

Monday, Rachel won't look my way, and I try not to look at her, either. I know she's embarrassed by what we saw at her place, and I don't know what to say to her about it. Just before we get on the bus to go home, though, she says, "If you want to interview me tomorrow, we could do it over the lunch period."

"Sure," I say. "I'll look for you." That's *something* to be happy about.

But when Dad comes home from work, he don't look all that happy and don't have much to say. Stands at the kitchen window drinking a glass of cold tea Ma left for him in the refrigerator, looking out over the yard.

"Hard day?" Ma asks, reaching into the cupboard.

Dad sighs. "Yeah . . ." He takes another drink of tea. Finally, "And I said something I shouldn't."

Don't know who he's talking to, but I look up from my homework there on the table. Ma takes down the cinnamon can and opens the lid. "What was that?" she says.

"Ed Sholt was raking leaves when I stopped at his box this afternoon, and you know how he's always felt about Judd. Well, he can't go on claiming that Judd set that fire when it's been proved how it started, so he says, 'Ray, somebody says you got folks living in a tent on your land. That true?' I can tell he's spoiling for a quarrel, so I just say, 'I got a guest camping there for a while.'"

Dad turns away from the window. "Ed says, 'Isn't there a regulation against that?' And . . . well, my back was hurting and I wasn't in any mood for that nonsense, so I say, 'If there is and your house ever burns down, Ed, I'll make sure you don't move in.'"

Ma gives him an exasperated look. "Oh, Ray . . . ," she says.

Dad goes on: "I just closed his box and drove off, but he yelled something after me, about keeping Shiloh away from his geese, or he'd come home full of buckshot."

Now I jump in the conversation: "Shiloh don't chase geese! He's a fraidy-cat when it comes to geese."

Ma leans back against the counter. "Ray, you know how quick-tempered Ed Sholt is. You didn't have to say what you did."

"Okay, I already said I shouldn't!" Now Dad turns on her. "What's done is done. I'm not afraid of Ed. I was just . . . thinking of Shiloh."

What if Shiloh really did chase his geese? I'm thinking. *What kind of life is it for a dog if you have to keep him inside all the time?*

I don't know how good an interview it'll be in a noisy cafeteria, all the hollering and laughing and chairs sliding in and out. David agrees it'll be a better interview if he's not there. Embarrassing enough for her to face the one of us.

There's a certain table in the cafeteria that nobody likes to sit at, right next to a table reserved for teachers. Only a couple kids there, so Rachel and I place our trays down at the other end. I decide right off I'm not going to mention the shed.

Get my notebook and pen ready. "Guess maybe I should find out where you lived before you moved out here," I tell her. "Can start with where you were born, if

121

you want." Then I take a bite of my ham and cheese and pick up my pen. Rachel just sits looking down at her chicken salad.

"It was because I was watching a program he didn't like," she says. And I know she's not going to let it pass.

"It's okay," I tell her. "I wasn't going to ask—"

But it's the shed she wants to talk about. "I don't see anything wrong with the program. The other girls are allowed to watch. When he found out I'd turned it on again, he pulled me out to the shed and locked me in it." She's speaking softly so nobody else can hear.

I take a big breath. "Rachel," I say. "It's none of my business, but has your dad ever hit you? Things like that?"

"I wish he *did* hit me!" she says, though I don't believe her. "I think I'd rather have that and get it over, than be told how I'm rotting my mind and disappointing my family and disobeying my father and losing my chance at heaven and . . ."

She picks up her fork and jabs at her salad like it's something evil. I take another bite of my sandwich, chewing in slow motion. Don't know what to say.

Rachel gives this little shrug. "Okay. Biography: We moved here from Weston. My dad had a church there for a while. I'm not sure where we lived before that—down around Hinton, I think. Ma told me once we've moved seven times since I was born. What else do you need to know?" Her words come out all choppy and cold.

"Well . . . what do you like to do when you're not in school? Any hobbies?" I ask.

Right off I can see her face relax some.

"Dance. I like all kinds of dance—ballet and modern and jazz. I just like moving to music," she says. "When both of my parents are out, I put on this CD and Ruthie and I dance together in my room. I wish I could take interpretive dancing. I saw that on TV once and really liked it."

"Maybe you'll turn out to be a dancer," I say, trying to think of something cheerful.

She looks at me like I just said pigs can sing. "Are you kidding? I can't even watch it on TV. Dad wouldn't let us go to the Halloween party because there might be dancing at it."

"Oh. Well, you ever go places on your own? I mean, do you have a bike?" I ask.

Rachel shakes her head. "Wish I did. I think about leaving all the time. Once I'm eighteen I will, maybe. But what would Ruthie do? She never fights back, so I do it for her."

"Your ma ever stick up for you?"

"She tries, but gives up. Never helps. You won't put any of this in the article, will you? About that, and the shed?"

"'Course not," I say. Then, changing the subject, "What's the worst part about moving to a new place? I never did."

"Having to start all over at everything," she says. "New school, new church, new dentist, new doctor . . . I have a lot of earaches, so a neighbor suggested a Dr. Murphy. Is he nice?"

"He's the best," I tell her. I start to say he stitched up my dog, but figure that's maybe not the right kind of recommendation to give out. For the rest of the lunch period she talks about the things she and her little sister like to do together—how she's teaching Ruthie to knit, and how once, in the last place they lived, they got this big piece of cardboard and used it to slide down a long, grassy hill. She's also started piano lessons.

I try to think of things that would make a good biography. Since I asked her all the things she likes, I ask her to name something she hates. Then I wish I hadn't, because she might think I'm trying to get her to answer, "My dad." But no.

"Having my picture taken," she says.

"Don't know why. You got nice teeth," I say, and that makes her laugh. She really does have a nice smile, just don't use it very much.

It's a long morning at Dr. Collins's clinic the Saturday before Thanksgiving. Dogs come in to be groomed, cats to be rid of matted-up hair on their bellies. Got a parrot losing its feathers, a snake—can't tell if it's dead or not. A rabbit's got an eye infection. . . .

"Everybody wants his pet looking nice for Thanksgiving," says Chris, the vet's assistant. He's studying to be a vet and says it takes a long time to pass all the tests.

You've got to know a lot to be a veterinarian. All humans have two eyes and ears and nostrils, two lungs and kidneys and arms and legs. All alike in that way. No feathers or scales or fur on any of 'em. But a whole lot of difference between a fish and a bird and a goat.

I probably work harder that morning than I ever have at the clinic. After I clean up the poop in the dog run, I put fresh towels in the cages, wash all the dishes in a special solution, and refill all the water bowls. I put fresh straw in a rabbit's cage and water in its bottle. I file records, answer the phone, make appointments, and check supplies in the cupboard.

Around twelve thirty, I see Dad waiting in the Jeep, so I get my jacket.

"I don't know what we'd have done without you today, Marty," Dr. Collins says.

"Well, I like doing it all," I tell him. "Except when an animal dies."

"I feel the same way," says Dr. Collins. And then, "I almost forgot. Someone brought in an injured dog a couple days ago. Hit by a car, and he died right here on the table. Hurt bad. A brown coon dog . . ." He goes to a cupboard and pulls out a drawer, but my stomach's already knotted up. "Had an old collar on him, but the letters were so worn I can't make out the name. Any idea who he belonged to?"

I know even before I look. It's a cheap fake leather collar, and the owner's name had been stamped on with some kind of machine in gold-colored lettering— *A . . . V . . . E . . . R . . .* is all I can make out, but I know right off it's Judd's.

"I'll take it to him," I say. "Judd Travers."

"You know him? Tell him we're sorry, but the dog had internal injuries and died before I could do anything for him." He shakes his head. "A dog runs free, these things happen."

eleven

I SURE AS HECK DIDN'T WANT THE JOB OF TELLING JUDD that one of his dogs was dead.

If this had been a couple of years ago, it could have been Judd himself who killed it in a fit over how it didn't snap to soon enough when he whistled. Like I said, he never even cared enough to give his dogs names. All he cared about was how they could help him hunt each fall. Now it was November—deer season—he don't even have a gun. Those burned up too. Only thing he goes in the woods for now is to find his dogs.

I think he first started to feel something for them back when I earned Shiloh from him; after Shiloh saved his life by letting us know Judd had run his truck into a ditch and was hurt bad; and then, when *he* saved *Shiloh*, by jumping in Middle Island Creek last spring when it turned into a river. After we fenced in Judd's backyard for him, giving his dogs a place to run instead of being chained, they got more playful. And now that they're gone, he misses a dog more than he ever thought he could.

I couldn't find my voice to tell Dr. Collins it was me who let those dogs out. I know he'd say it was better than letting them burn—I was giving them a chance. But I never thought they'd get all the way down here to St. Mary's.

When Dad picks me up, I tell him how worried I am of what Judd might do, he finds out one of his dogs got run over—start drinkin' and drivin' crazy. . . .

"Marty, where you get the idea you're responsible for what Judd does or don't do?" says Dad. "He's had problems before you ever came along. Judd's a grown man— got to make his own choices."

I guess I'm worrying Judd might get the idea that he give up Shiloh too soon and want him back again— that Shiloh once and always will belong to him, no matter what, especially since I'm the one let those dogs out.

On the way home I'm wrestling with why I didn't ask Dr. Collins if he'd seen the white dog around there somewhere, and what I should do next. Make some posters about the missing dog, that's one thing I haven't tried. But first, I got to face Judd.

When there's bad news to be told, though, I think it's better to come right out with it; the more disguises you put on it, the bigger the shock when it jumps out at you.

So I'm waiting out on the porch when Judd gets home from Whelan's. Ma's left him a big piece of caramel cake, and I watch him park his truck and walk over.

I hand him the foil-wrapped package and say, "Got some bad news, Judd. It's about your brown dog." And then, when I see his face is ready for the worst, that's what I give him: "He got hit by a car down near St. Mary's a few days ago."

Judd's face freezes into a stone-eyed, twisted look, and then he sits down slow on the steps. "He die?"

I hate telling him, but I gotta. "Yeah. Somebody picked him up and brought him into the clinic where I help out on Saturdays. Dr. Collins says he died almost as soon as they got him in. He was hurt bad—internal injuries. We're all real sorry to hear about it." I hand him the dog collar, too.

Don't know how long Judd plans to sit on the steps,

'cause they are cold. It's almost Thanksgiving, and temperature's in the twenties. But he's sittin' there, cake in one hand, collar in the other, staring at those fading letters of his last name on the fake leather.

"What'd they do with the body?" he asks finally, voice all husky.

"I . . . don't know. Disposed of it, I guess . . . didn't know who it belonged to."

For a minute I'm afraid he'll get up, drive to the animal clinic, and cause some kind of trouble—something he might used to have done when he was drunk—but he just nods.

"Anybody see the other dog? My terrier?"

"N-not that I know of. Nothin' said about another dog."

"They'd be runnin' around together, wouldn't you think?"

"Could be. But I'm going to make some posters to put up, Judd. And I'll write our phone number on them, in case anyone sees him."

Judd just sits there all hunched over, and I'm thinkin' maybe I ought to go inside. Not polite to stand around watching a man grieve. But Judd goes on, "Had me five dogs once. Killed one by accident; one on purpose; let you have the third; the fourth's been run over, and the fifth's just run off, I guess. It's a sorry state when a man can't even keep his own dogs. Can't say I deserved 'em, though."

He gets up finally, collar in hand, and heads for the tent. Leaves the cake behind on the steps.

I think all of us thought the dogs would be back by now. Thought they were just having a fine time running free, and when they got really hungry, they'd be back to the only place they'd known as home. And that when they found it all burned down, they'd follow Judd's scent over here. Never thought they'd get so far away. What will the white one do now that his buddy's gone? Hard to put my brain in the mind of a dog.

The next day Dad puts on his work clothes and goes across the creek to help haul away more of those burned-out walls and furniture and car engines. Once again, I can see he's not fixing to work on our new addition, so I go to church with Ma and the girls.

Just like last Sunday, Rachel sits there beside her ma and Ruthie, still as a post. Nobody would guess she's a girl her daddy locked in a shed. From where I sit, I don't see her look at her dad even once. Got her eyes down on the hymnbook or out the windows. He can make her go to church but can't make her look at him.

I'm thinking maybe she sits there every Sunday figuring how in six more years she's going to leave home, nobody coming after her, neither.

Preacher must have heard what Judd said at Wallace's store, 'cause he's on blasphemy this Sunday. I didn't even know what the word meant until he'd repeated it about nine times.

"Brothers and sisters, don't be deceived by those who blaspheme against you and this church, those who have never even set foot in this church," he says.

And I'm pretty sure the women in Wallace's store have told the preacher about me mouthing off to them too, because a little later he reads a verse from the Bible prophesying that this is the kind of behavior we can expect among the godless.

"Isaiah, chapter three, verse five," he says. "'And the people shall be oppressed, every one by another, and every one by his neighbor; the child shall behave himself proudly against the ancient, and the base against the honorable.'" And he warns that those who stand idly by and do not defend the church when sinners revile it are just as guilty as if the words came out of their own mouths, for if you are not *for* the Church of the Everlasting Life, then you must be against it.

I guess this sermon is meant for the likes not only of

Judd Travers and me, but the preacher's very own daughters.

You can see his preaching's made a difference, though. Looks to me like most of the families who'd been saying that maybe Judd set the fire—the Sholts and the Nileses and the Robinsons and the Peterses—are on one side of the church, and the Herndons, the Jacksons, the Murphys and the Frisks—the ones who believe the newspaper, not the gossip—are on the other, the same people who had a good word for Judd after he rescued my dog.

Back when Pastor Evans was here, didn't we all mostly sit together? I try to remember. When there was a potluck supper, didn't we all dig in?

This time when the service is over, Rachel don't turn her head away when she sees me.

"Hi, Marty," she says quietly.

"Hi," I tell her. I may know more about Rachel Dawes than her parents suspect, but her secrets are safe with me.

That afternoon Ma finds us some spare sheets of white paper and colored markers, and we set about making lost-dog posters.

No use asking Judd if he'd taken any pictures of his white dog, because even if he had, they all burned up in the fire. Dara Lynn's pretty good when it comes to drawing, and she takes a black marker and makes the outline of a white dog on some of the pages, just a dog's head on the others.

Becky fusses that she wants to do something, so I make the *L* and the *D* of the Lost Dog words big two-sided letters and see if she can color inside the lines. Then we get the idea to use a glue stick between the lines on some of the posters, and the girls sprinkle their left-over red sparkles from Valentine's Day over the letters, then tip the papers so the extra sparkles fall off into the wastebasket. Nice and bright. Nobody's going to miss *these* signs.

It's what to say about the dog that stumps us. When a dog don't have a name and you don't know of any special spots on him, don't help to make things up. We hear Judd's truck coming back from somewhere, and I go call him to come inside.

"We're making dog posters!" Becky tells him, and holds up one of the sparkle pictures. I can tell by the scrunch of his eyebrows that Judd's havin' a hard time connectin' the red sparkles to his terrier.

"Sit down, Judd. Won't you take some coffee and pie?" Ma says.

"Well . . . coffee anyway, thanks. Keep the pie till

later, maybe," he tells her. Shiloh comes over, sniffs at Judd's boots, then goes back and lies down on the floor between the girls' chairs.

"Help us describe him, Judd," I say. "Every little detail you can think of."

Judd unzips his jacket and stares some more at the papers scattered around the table. "Well, he was white," he says.

"Didn't he have a patch of gray behind his left ear?" I ask.

Judd tries hard to remember. "Might have. He'd always . . . uh . . . circle his supper dish when he was eating . . . or was that the coon dog?"

I have my pencil handy, waiting to write something down, but nothing comin' I can use. Dara Lynn lays her head down on one arm and makes little scribbles on one of the papers. "Big or little?" she asks.

"A medium-size dog," says Judd.

Ma sets the cup of coffee in front of him, and we all wait. Becky puts a spot of glue on the back of her hand and drops a pinch of sparkles on it. Then she holds out her hand and grins. "Do you like this, Shiloh?" she says, dangling it in front of Shiloh's nose.

Shiloh looks up, sniffs at the glue, and lays his head back down again.

"You might could say this," Judd says at last. "When I'd sit on the back step with my knees bent, he liked to crawl in the space under my legs and curl up there."

Hmmm, I'm thinking. "Anything else?" I ask.

"When he slept, sometimes he'd dream, and his front paws would jerk, you know . . . like he's trackin' something in the woods. . . ."

Judd looks tired, and I know he's probably not sleeping a lot.

"Well," I tell him, "I'll take a poster down to Dr. Collins's clinic, and I'll ask Mrs. Wallace if she'd put one up in her store window too. I been tellin' everyone I see to call us if there's a stray white dog nosing around."

"Thanks, Marty," Judd says. "And thanks for the coffee and pie," he tells Ma, reaching for the little package. He zips his jacket up again. Then he takes one last look at the red sparkle posters, gives Becky a weary smile, and goes on out to the tent.

It's a potluck Thanksgiving. Ma and the preacher's wife and some of the other women have done their best to make that basement room at the church look like home. Got curtains along one wall, not even any windows on it, and some pictures here and there.

A couple of donated couches sit at one end with

orange and black and red pillows on them to brighten things up. Three long folding tables with as many chairs as we can squeeze around them fill up the rest of the floor space, and at the other end is the fourth table filled with homemade food brought in that morning.

Only got room for the families of those burned-out houses who been staying at the Mountain View Motel till their insurance money comes. Them and the families of the women and men who organized this dinner. Want to make the motel families feel like guests in somebody's home. Ma said she invited Judd Travers, but after that sermon the Sunday before, probably a good thing he don't show up.

Dara Lynn and Ruthie manage to sit together, and I'm between Doc Murphy and Mr. Beringer. Doc's wife died a few years back, and he takes every opportunity to eat home-cooked food. As he lifts a fork to his mouth, I see the back of his hand all covered with brown spots, the way I remember Grandma Preston's hands.

"You know, Marty," he says, "I was going over my account book the other day, and you're about paid up with what you owe me. I figure another hour should do it."

That's the best thing that's happened to me in months! Been over a year now, and every couple weeks

I've gone to Doc Murphy's to see what he had for me to do. Hearing that I'm almost paid up is what Ma calls a hallelujah day. I smile and reach for a piece of pecan pie to celebrate.

Someone across the table asks Sam Beringer what he's planning to do now that his house burned down.

"I got to get me a car before I can do much of anything," he says. "I was so low on gas I'd asked Judd to get me a gallon before he come home from work the day the fire broke out. He brought it, all right, but by then I didn't have a car to put it in or a house neither. The only way to go now, I guess, is up."

That night the girls are watching *How the Grinch Stole Christmas*, and Ma and Dad are still at the table. I've pulled my chair over to the doorway, waiting for the program to be over so I can have the TV next, and Ma and Dad go on talking in low voices.

"I haven't learned very much from Judith about how they discipline their girls. Couldn't seem to find the right time to bring it up," Ma's saying. "She did say that Jacob can't accept that they don't always obey when he tells them to do something, and he can be harsh sometimes, is the way she put it. I managed to say that one of the most important things I've learned as a parent is that your children obey better if they want to please you, not if they're afraid of you."

And Dad asks, "What'd she say to that?"

Ma answers, "I don't know that she said anything. She's a quiet kind of woman, Ray. I wouldn't be surprised if *she's* not afraid of him too."

One of the most important things *I've* learned about as a *kid* is that if you pretend to be concentrating really hard on something—your homework or a puzzle or the TV or something—grown-ups will talk about all kinds of things they wouldn't say if they knew you were listening. . . .

twelve

SCHOOL'S CLOSED THE FRIDAY AFTER THANKSGIVING, and everybody's gone to the nearest Walmart or Sears to start their Christmas shopping. Roads up around where we live more empty than ever. We get only one call about a white dog hanging around, but just as I'm fixing to go looking for it, the woman phones back and says she found out it was a neighbor's dog down the way, sorry to have bothered us.

Laura calls, though, to say that a couple trash cans got knocked over where she lives, somewhere between Little and Friendly. Could have been a hungry dog looking for dinner. There's a fair-size patch of woods in there, so after I have breakfast, I take Shiloh, get on my bike, and head out. Get to the woods and walk my bike down into the gully behind some gooseberry bushes, and then we set off.

A new woods to a dog must be like a Sunday buffet. Can't hardly decide what smell to try next, tail awagging like a windshield wiper.

"Wait, Shiloh," I say if he looks to be getting too far ahead. He'll lope back again, but I don't think he understands the meaning of words; I think it's the tone of voice. So I test him on it. Next time he gets too far ahead, I say, "Wait, poop-breath," and back he comes.

One of us has got to keep our directions straight, though, or we'll both get lost. Knew the woods on Judd's side of the creek better than I know these. And Shiloh don't even know what we're looking for. Comes to a scattering of deer poop and starts to roll over in it. I yell at him so fast he's on his feet again, nose to the ground. See whatever nasty he can come upon next. Here's another *why*: Why does a dog who can be so loving like to smell so bad?

Been tramping through the woods an hour or more, and suddenly I realize the sun's been clouded over a good long while. Feel the first drop of rain on my cheek and then, after a bit, another. I know it's time—past time—to go home.

Shiloh's gone on ahead, and I give a call. Can hear the rustle of underbrush as he noses about, and I turn around. Give a whistle. More raindrops. Big ones, and I am going to be soaked by the time I get home.

"C'mon, Shiloh!" I yell, and I start to run, making my way back through the trees. I whistle again when I reach the road and haul my bike up out of the bushes.

But Shiloh hasn't come, and this time I yell at the top of my voice, "Shiloh! Get yourself out here!"

If I can't make him come, the rain will, cause Shiloh hates rain, so I ride on home, my head down as far as I can tip it and still see the pavement in front of me. It's a cold rain too, not like the warm summer rain we waited on for so long. And when I pedal up our lane and drag my bike up on the porch, I am soaked through.

"Looks like somebody got caught in a cloudburst," Ma says. "Better leave your clothes right there on the porch and I'll bring you some clean ones."

While I change, I tell her about checking out the woods.

"Shiloh's still out there," I say.

"Well, you know he hates rain, so he's probably under a bush or someone's porch and will be along when it quits," Ma tells me.

There's turkey noodle soup for supper, and pumpkin pie with Cool Whip on top. Dad tells us about how much holiday traffic there was down on Route 2, how he couldn't wait to make the turn at the Friendly post office and head up into the hills where we live.

"I get to the Jennings place, though, and her mailbox is all torn down and chewed up," Dad says. "Linda comes out to the box to tell me she put a piece of mince pie in there the night before. Had it all wrapped up in foil and figured it would be safe in a metal mailbox till I got there the next day. In the night, the raccoons knocked the post over, she thinks, and clawed open that box, all for a piece of mince pie."

We laugh, and Dad says, "Told her my stomach was already full from Thanksgiving dinner, but she had another piece all wrapped up to give me. Told me if I saw any raccoons on the road, she wouldn't mind if I ran 'em over, 'cause they've been particularly mean this year."

"Did you run over any, Daddy?" asks Becky.

"No, sugar. I don't run over anything 'less it's an accident."

I get this bad feeling about Shiloh and raccoons. "Where do the Jennings live?" I ask.

"Oh, 'bout halfway between Little and Friendly. Just before that patch of woods on the right," says Dad.

Same patch of woods I was in that afternoon. And suddenly I don't want the rest of my pumpkin pie. Shiloh's not new to raccoons, of course. Must have seen plenty around our place. But . . . what do you really know about what your dog does when you're not with him? You can say he don't mess with raccoons and he don't chase geese, but how you going to prove that? I've seen animals brought into Dr. Collins's clinic that have been in fights with raccoons, so how do I know what Shiloh was sniffing out when he had his nose there on the ground in that woods?

Tonight the girls are watching *A Charlie Brown Christmas*, but I don't much feel like watching. Seen that about a dozen times in my life already, and after they've gone to bed, I'd rather keep the TV off so I can hear if Shiloh's scratching at the door. I leave the porch light on so I can look out from time to time, but the porch stays as empty as I feel inside.

"You still worrying about Shiloh?" Ma asks. "He'll be along. You know that."

She's probably right. Tomorrow he'll come trotting up to the house like, *what was all the fuss about?*

When I settle down on the couch with my blanket and pillow, I feel another *why* coming on. Why is it humans and animals can't communicate with each other—some kind of language, I mean? Like, I could ask Shiloh all kinds of questions, and he'd bark once for yes and two for no. That kind of talking. Man, I'd give him the third degree when he got back.

I dream of Shiloh that night. Dream that I throw open the door and say, "I *knew* you'd be back!" But when I wake Saturday morning, listening for sounds in the kitchen, I know right off that if Shiloh was there, he'd be panting his dog breath in my face. I turn away and pull my arms up around my head.

Eat hardly anything for breakfast. Get on my bike and ride back to that woods, calling every ten seconds, and I think I walk all the way through to the other side, 'cause I see houses on up ahead.

I go home around noon so Mom'll know where I've been, but got no appetite for lunch. I know Shiloh's been away all night once or twice before, but I try to remember if he ever wasn't back by the next morning. Get on my bike and check both sides of the road again, calling all the while. Not a sign of Shiloh anywhere.

When I get home a second time, there's Christmas music playing on the radio and a fire going in our pot-bellied stove. Ma's starting in on the seven different kinds of Christmas cookies she makes each year, keeping them in metal tins in the bottom of our refrigerator till all of them are baked. Then she'll take them around to friends and neighbors. Dara Lynn and Becky are there at the table, putting almonds in the tops of little round balls of dough, or chocolate sprinkles on cookies of a different kind. I finally eat the lunch Ma put aside for me, but it's just to stop the ache in my belly.

If Shiloh don't never come back, Christmas won't feel like Christmas. Even if I had me a bedroom all to myself, what's the joy in it without Shiloh there on top of my feet? Licking my face to wake me up in the morning? Can't believe he isn't back by now.

Becky stops her cookie decorating and comes into the living room to give me a wordless hug, head on my lap, then goes back to the table. Even Dara Lynn keeps her sassiness to herself. Ma gives her an orange in the afternoon, and she peels it open, gives half to me.

All I can think about at dinner are the bad things that could have happened to my dog. Gettin' run over, like Judd's. Tore up again by the German shepherd. What if it really was Shiloh and the black Lab running through Ed Sholt's yard, scattering the geese, and he took a shotgun to Shiloh like he threatened? Who would blame him? I should have learned from Dr. Collins all the things that can happen to pets when you let 'em run free.

But Shiloh's run free ever since I got him. Always used to the great outdoors. And that's what I tell Dad later when he comes out and stands on the porch beside me in the dark.

"Same with children, Marty," he says. "When you're young, just a baby, we're watchin' you all the while, keeping you safe. But comes a time you're going to go places we can't go with you, ride in cars with someone else driving, take chances, be silly, make choices. And more'n once your ma's said to me she wishes she could bubble-wrap her kids, keep 'em safe wherever they go. But we can't. And that's no kind of life at all."

"But you can talk to your children," I argue. "You can tell them where it's safe to play and where it's not. Dogs don't understand." I can feel the corners of my mouth tugging down. I wipe one hand across my cheek.

"That's true," Dad agrees.

So what am I arguing for? To fence him in? "I helped Judd fence his yard in once," I say miserably.

Dad looks down at me. "A dog that's used to running all over creation would need a pretty big yard," he says.

"We could do it, though, with chicken wire. Keep him there till I got home from school each day, and then I could take him out. If Shiloh comes back," I promise, "I'll work just like I did for Doc Murphy to earn money to buy those fence posts and chicken wire. I'll help dig the postholes, like we did for Judd's dogs, and we can stretch it to go behind the oak trees out back, so he can chase squirrels around 'em, and whenever I'm on my

147

bike, Shiloh can go along, and even when David Howard comes over, we'll take Shiloh wherever we go. . . ."

Dad's shakin' his head, ever so slight, but he says, "Well, we'll see, Marty." And even I realize it don't make a lot of sense, 'cause I was right there with Shiloh yesterday, and he still disappeared.

Besides, nothing I promise myself brings him back. Suppertime comes, and if Shiloh was around, he'd be here, begging. Tomorrow's Sunday. He's been gone over twenty-four hours now. I imagine making posters about Shiloh. *Two* dogs missing.

When Judd stops by, Ma tells him about Shiloh.

"Well, that's a heck of a thing!" Judd says. Then, trying to make me feel better, I guess, he says, "But Shiloh knows the way home, Marty. My dog don't even have a home."

That don't cheer me much.

"I'll keep my eye out for him," he promises, and goes on out to the tent.

"Do you think we could get up early tomorrow, Dad, and go out in the car looking?" I ask, trying to keep my voice from cracking.

"Yes, I think we could do that," he answers.

I go outside and whistle for Shiloh one last time before bed. Stand there waiting for the rustle in the bushes, Shiloh coming home. Nothing but the silence of stars, looking down at me.

Don't seem like the right way to go about it, but I'm wondering, should I go to church tomorrow? Like maybe if God sees me in church, he'll bring Shiloh back. Still . . . First off, if God knows everything we're thinking, he'll know I pulled on my Sunday pants and my shirt with the stiff collar just in case it would bring my dog back. And God don't like phony.

Second, if I pray and ask him to bring Shiloh home, it's like God took him, maybe. At least, that he knows where Shiloh's at and has the power to bring him back.

And third, do I want to pray to a God who took my dog? And if he's got the power to bring him back, why don't he just do it? Why do we have to beg?

I'm in and out of sleep, only barely aware that Dad's making himself some coffee in the kitchen, pouring himself a bowl of cereal and making toast.

Then I feel his hand on my shoulder, nudging me awake. Remembering we're going to go look for Shiloh.

"All right," I say, trying to keep my eyes open. "I'm coming."

But I'm back in my dream, my head sinking deep in the pillow. I feel Dad shaking my shoulder again.

"Marty," Dad keeps saying. "Get up. Want to show you something."

I sit up in a snap and look around for Shiloh. But he's not here. Still, I haul myself up off the couch and follow Dad over to the window next to our table.

"Look out there," he says.

It's barely light, and I rub my eyes. Can just make out the trees and shed and chicken coop.

"What?" I ask.

"Look over at Judd's tent."

I lean a little closer and stare hard.

Right outside the zipped-up door flap is a white dog, head on its paws.

And standing off to the other side . . . is Shiloh.

thirteen

CAN'T HARDLY BELIEVE MY EYES.

"Shiloh!" I shout, and whirl around so fast I'm like to lose my balance, arms going like windmills to keep me upright as I start for the door.

But Dad reaches out and stops me.

"Wait!" he says. "Look here a minute. Judd's got his lantern on now. I want you to see this."

"But Shiloh!" I say again.

"He's not goin' anywhere. Don't ruin this for Judd," Dad tells me.

The next sixty seconds is the longest minute I ever spent in my life, just watching that white dog waiting for Judd, and Shiloh out there wagging his tail.

"Shiloh brought Judd's dog back, didn't he?" I say.

"Sure looks that way," says Dad, huge smile on his face.

Bein' Sunday, Judd don't have to go to work, but most Sundays he hangs out at a diner over in Middlebourne. He'll pull on his clothes, splash water on his face at the pump, then drive to a take-out place for coffee.

"C'mon, c'mon, Judd," I say, my eyes on Shiloh. Sure don't want to lose my dog again. Not easy for a man to get dressed inside a tent, I suppose. Ma washes his clothes, but he keeps them out there, and I figure they're as stiff and frosty as the air when he puts 'em on.

Now the light goes out and we see the tent flap open. First dog Judd sees is Shiloh. Turns his head and sees the terrier. Then we hear Judd shout.

He's crouched there on his hands and knees, staring at that dog, on its feet now looking back at him, tail picking up speed. Then the terrier's in Judd's arms, licking him all over his face.

One second later I'm out on the porch in my pajamas—barefoot, too—and almost before I can call his name, Shiloh's racing 'cross the yard, lickety-split, piling on top of me, licking me up one side the head, down the other.

"Oh, Shiloh!" I say, hugging him tight. "Shiloh!"

"Marty," I hear Judd call. "Look what I got! He come back to me!"

"Shiloh brought him!" I shout, and the both of us are showing off our dogs like it's Christmas morning already. Judd Travers don't often give a full 100 percent happy kind of smile, but if he ever did, this one's it.

"Well, get in here, the four of you," Dad says, holding the door open wide, and both dogs skitter across the linoleum. "So you got your dog back, Judd! Sure can tell you were missing each other. Come sit down and have some breakfast."

I'm already reaching for the sack of dog food. I pour two bowls' full, and I see Judd's dog so thin his ribs are showing. His legs tremble a little as he eats, and Judd can't take his eyes off him.

"All this time, and he come back to me," he says. "I'm going to take him around, show him off to some of the fellas in Middlebourne. Maybe buy him a barbecue sandwich at the diner. I'll put me a blanket in my truck, and he can sleep there all day to stay warm."

I can't wait for Shiloh to finish eating, so I can hug him again.

Ma comes out in the kitchen in her robe. "Well, for goodness' sake, look here!" she says, her eyes traveling from Judd's dog to Shiloh. "When did all this happen?"

"'Bout five minutes ago," I tell her. "Shiloh brought Judd's dog back, and they were waiting outside the tent for Judd to wake up." I find two pans and give both dogs some fresh water, and they lap it up, drops flying every which way.

"Well, let me fix some breakfast for you, Judd," says Ma.

"No, I'm on my way to Middlebourne, but thank you," says Judd. "Going to keep my dog company all day." And when his dog has finished eating, Judd scoops him up in his arms again and off they go together.

"That's a happy ending if I ever saw one," says Dad, taking his bread out of the toaster and buttering it up.

"Ending to what?" I ask.

"Oh, to this chapter of Judd's life, I guess—losing his trailer home and his other dog." He points to the second piece of toast. "Want it?"

I reach over, and take the jelly jar, too, and Ma goes off to take a shower. I'm full awake now—awake enough to eat breakfast with Dad, anyway. Feeling pretty good about my dad right then, so I say, "Any chance we can finish the new addition by Christmas?"

Dad puts down his spoon. "Marty, I know you were really counting on that. But I've got to put in the insulation, the electric, the ceiling, the drywall, the heat—and we don't even have a doorway yet, connecting it to the dining room."

That's a no if I ever heard one. Don't know what I was hoping he'd say. That he'd take his two-week vacation now and spend it all working on the house, just so I can have a room of my own by Christmas? Hate to admit it, but what's really going on in my head is that he's been helping out folks across the creek the past couple Sundays when he could have been working over here.

"It's like this, Marty. Our family's not squeezed into a motel room. You're the one having to sleep on the couch, I know, and you've been looking forward to your own room for a long time. But there are kids in that motel who just want a real place to call home. And if I can get them there a little faster by helping clear their land, I think I ought to do it."

Didn't hear nothing I didn't expect. Feeling sorry for myself, I guess. Wanted Dad to at least say he's sorry we won't have that room done by Christmas. He don't. Saving his sorry for the folks who got burned out.

"You understand?" Dad says at last, finishing the rest of his coffee.

"Yeah," I say. I don't have to like it, but I understand, and wish I hadn't asked the question. Should have held on to my Shiloh happiness a little longer before I brought the subject up.

Girls can't hardly wait for Judd to get back that night, 'cause they've both got names for his dog. Judd's spent the day watching football with a friend, and his pickup pulls in about eight, girls already in their pajamas.

I call out, ask him to come on in, Ma's got some white beans on the stove waiting. So he does.

"Where's the dog?" I ask.

"One of the mechanics from Whelan's has a fenced-in yard. Says he'll keep him for me till I get a pen of my own," Judd says. Unzips his jacket, and Ma slides a plate onto the table.

"Well, that worked out well, didn't it?" says Ma, glad, I know, there won't be an extra dog here.

"Yeah, fellas have all been pretty good to me," Judd says, and sits down. "This here looks mighty good. Thank you."

"We've picked out some names for your dog!" Dara Lynn says eagerly. "You want to hear them?"

"You're thinkin' of naming my dog?"

"Yes!" says Becky. "Fluffy."

"Fluffy?" says Judd. "What kind of name is that for a dog?"

Becky sticks out her lower lip and turns toward Dara Lynn to hear her idea.

"I think you should call him Lucky, because he's lucky he didn't get run over," she tells him.

"He's lucky all right," says Judd.

"Pal would be a nice name for him, now that he's come back," says Ma.

"Well, he's already got a name. I named him this morning," says Judd. "Norman."

"Norman?" we all say together. What kind of name is *that* for a dog?

"It's my middle name," says Judd.

What could we say? But I think we knew right then that Judd was going to take good care of that dog, now that it was a member of his family.

"Been a fine day. Norman must be good luck for me," he says, enjoying the beans. "I drove over to another man's house, showed off my dog—they all know he's been missing—and he's got a trailer I can use for a while."

"Well, hey!" says Dad.

"Only big enough for a squirrel, but he keeps it in his yard for relatives' visits. Got people coming for

Christmas, but he says I can move it over on my property after the first of the year, and keep it till I can buy
something bigger."

"That's wonderful, Judd," says Ma.

"I got some money saved up, and I'm thinking of
getting me one of those prefabricated two-room houses,"
Judd says.

"The kind you put together yourself?" asks Dad.

"That's the kind," Judd tells him. "Maybe we could
help each other out. I could help with your insulation
and all, and you could maybe help me put up the frame
for my house when it comes. Two rooms should be big
enough for me and Norman."

And we all think that's a fine idea.

Christmas itself is big in our family, but presents aren't.
The same time Dad was paying medical bills for his ma,
we've been trying to save up to buy the materials for that
extra room on our house.

Last year was the hardest for us—Uncle Bill had lost
his house in a flood, and of course we didn't need a dog
to care for too, but that's when I brung home Shiloh.

"Poorest we've ever been, that one year," Ma says.

We don't have two cars, so no way she could get a
job, and even if she could, she's got Becky to care for,

not in school yet. So that year she told Dara Lynn and me not to expect much for Christmas, and on Christmas morning we each of us found a card with a five-dollar bill in it, and a package under the tree: a giant-size box each of our own favorite cereal, nobody could eat it but us. Becky, of course, with that super-size box of Froot Loops, carried it around to announce it was all for her. But Dara Lynn still remembers last year as the Cap'n Crunch Christmas.

Things are easier this year, but we're still being careful. I do my part by helping out at the animal clinic, so Dr. Collins takes care of any problem Shiloh's got for free. Didn't have to pay for the presents I'm giving my family either. Every one of them has John Collins's name on them. He gives them out to his clients at Christmas 'cause they're good advertising.

I got a little toy mouse for Dara Lynn to give her cat, and a paperback book about owls for Becky; both of them got JOHN COLLINS ANIMAL CLINIC stamped on them somewhere. Picked up a red plastic water dish for Shiloh, a rawhide bone for Judd to give to Norman, a hand towel for Ma with a paw-print design, and a JCAC key chain for Dad with a little jackknife and a flashlight on it.

Ma tells Judd she expects him to be here for Christmas

dinner. Tells him our aunt Hettie will be here too, and asks could he bring some firewood, which he's glad to do. Dr. Collins says humans and dogs are alike that way: want to know you count on them for something.

Dara Lynn and I have already chosen what tree we want Dad to chop down for us to decorate. Now that deer season is over, and we don't have to worry about somebody shooting on our seventy acres—which they do sometimes, even though we got them posted—we always go off and look for the biggest and best fir tree we can find.

But Dad surprises us on Tuesday by coming home from his mail route with a big bag from JCPenney, and of course we've practically got our noses in it before he takes off his jacket.

"Decided to do my Christmas shopping early this year," he says. "So Lou, here's your present, but I expect you'll share it with the whole family."

Ma's so surprised all she can do is watch as he reaches into the bag and pulls out a set of those icicle lights you see in catalogs, and then another, and another, till there's four sets laying there on the table. Dara Lynn and I give a shout when we see what they are.

"Oh, Ray, those are expensive!" Ma says, but I can tell by the smile lines on her face that she's happy about it.

Dad's grinning too. "I know we wanted our addition done by Christmas, but no reason we can't decorate what we have, is there?" he asks.

Now we're in the spirit! All we've had in the past is a tree with red and blue and green lights on it, and another string of red and green and blue around the door frame. That and a wreath on the door. But this . . . wow!

It's starting to get dark, but we can't wait one minute to put those lights up, so we bring out the stepladder. Ma and the girls have carefully uncoiled the lights, and with me holding a flashlight, Dad's screwing cup hooks along the edge of the porch roof, up the little diamond-shaped peak above the front door, and then on down the rest of the way under the eaves.

Judd drives up in his truck just then, and pretty soon Ma's handing a string of lights to him. Judd hands it up to Dad, and he starts looping it over the hooks at one end of the porch roof. I keep the flashlight aimed at wherever it's needed most. When that string is up, the little jiggery icicle lights hanging down all along the eaves, Ma hands up the second set; Dad connects it to the first and takes it all the way to the top of the peak. Then he starts down the other side with the third set, and finally, with a little adjusting, the fourth set is connected, the end hanging down.

It's a big project, 'cause if you plug too many in the same outlet, you could blow a fuse. But finally we got the stepladder moved out of the way, and Ma's standing in the doorway, her hand on the porch light switch.

"Everybody ready?" she calls, and we're all out there in the yard facing the house, like folks waiting for a flag to go up.

"Ready, set, go!" says Dad.

It's like our front porch turned into a fairyland. Becky shrieks and Dara Lynn oohs and even Judd Travers gives a whistle.

Ma comes out to enjoy it with us. "That is just the prettiest thing!" she says, over and over.

Tiny trickles of light, like dripping water, dance in the wind, sparkling and twinkling. Didn't ever know our house could look so beautiful.

"Do you think they can see us clear out on the road down as far as the bend?" asks Dara Lynn. "Can anybody over there the other side of the bridge see it, do you think?"

And when Ma tells her yes, they can see it from far off, she wants to know if people will drive all the way up from Friendly to see the Prestons' Christmas house. Guess we haven't driven that girl around enough at Christmas to think it's all *that* special.

At dinner the next night, we're all talking about Judd naming his dog Norman. Judd Norman Travers. Never heard Judd's full name before. But I guess it's his business. Just like I was the one who named Shiloh, Judd could name his dog whatever he liked.

"Ruthie hates her name," Dara Lynn says, and flips over her pork chop, like maybe it'll look better on the other side. She don't much care for meat.

"Dara Lynn, will you please quit bothering that chop and eat it?" says Dad.

"Why does she hate her name?" asks Becky, giving Dara Lynn a chance to fool around a while longer.

"Because her dad keeps telling her she was named after a famous woman in the Bible who was helpful to other people, and when Ruthie doesn't obey, he tells her she's not being 'Ruth-like.' She wants to change her name to Rocky."

Dad thinks that's funny. Ma laughs too.

"When I was little, I wanted to change my name from Louanne to Stephanie," Ma tells us.

"Why?" asks Becky.

"I don't know. Just liked it, I guess."

But Dara Lynn's losing our attention, so she says, "Whenever Ruthie's being bad at the table, she used to have to sit in the 'thinking chair.'"

"The 'thinking chair'?" says Dad. "Wish I had one of those!"

"No, you don't!" says Dara Lynn. "It had clamps on the arms, and Ruthie had to sit with her wrists fastened—couldn't even scratch her nose—while everybody else ate."

"Dara Lynn!" scolds Ma. "Quit making things up!"

I've stopped chewing.

"It's true!" says Dara Lynn. "Once she even had to sit in it during supper just because she said a cuss word, and her dad said if she couldn't use her mouth for what God intended, she couldn't use it for eating, neither. She could sit and think about it, and watch the rest of them eat."

"What kind of chair has clamps on the arms?" asks Dad.

"I don't *know*!" Dara Lynn says. "That's all Ruthie told me. But she said she and Rachel hated that chair so much that one day Rachel threw it in the creek. The next time her dad wanted to use it, it was gone, and she wouldn't tell him where it was. She got locked in her room for a whole day and a whole night, and finally she told, but when they went to look for it, it had disappeared."

"Dara Lynn, if you are making up that story—" Ma begins.

I push away from the table. "She's not making it up," I say.

I pull on my jacket, take a flashlight, and go out the door, around the chicken coop to the old shed we keep our junk in. I open the door and haul out that chair David and I pulled from the creek. Brush off the dust and mice dirt and carry it back into the house.

Then I set it there beside the table. "This is it," I say.

fourteen

Everybody's staring at it.

"It's just like she said," Dara Lynn cries, and jumps up to go sit in it.

"Where did you get that, Marty?" asks Dad.

"David and I found it in the creek when we were looking for bottles and cans," I tell him. "I was going to use it for Halloween for a Frankenstein man in the laboratory." Dara Lynn's already trying the crab claws nailed to the ends. She puts an arm in one, pulls real hard, and the clamp opens. "I can get right out of here," she says.

"I can't believe this!" says Ma.

"I wanna try it!" says Becky, and she slides down out of her chair and runs over.

"Girls! Dara Lynn! Get yourself out of that chair!" says Ma.

Dara Lynn gets out and pulls Becky away. "We can't sit in it, Becky. It's Ruthie's."

"Oh, my goodness! It's nobody's, Becky!" Ma tells her. "It was thrown away and it's going to stay thrown away. I think it's disgusting. Get back up there and finish your dinner."

Dad pats me on the arm. "Go put it back, Marty, and we'll talk about it later."

"Later" is when the girls are making marshmallow-toothpick snowmen at the table, and Dad and Ma are in the living room, the TV turned low. They don't mind that I'm there.

"Maybe it's time to report this, Lou. The chair as evidence?" Dad says.

Ma's got one hand over her mouth. "Maybe so. But . . . oh, Ray! What it would do to Judith and the church!"

"Well, you're the one wanting to report it up till now. You want to hold back just 'cause he's a preacher?"

"No. If it's wrong for everybody, it's wrong for the preacher, too. And if we don't . . . Ruthie's so little and vulnerable—probably why Dara Lynn's so fond of her, a second grader."

Dad stretches out his legs and runs one hand through his hair. "I don't know . . . it's a tricky thing. Dawes seems to be just on the edge of what's legal and what's not. You give a child the choice of sitting out dinner in that chair or being spanked, maybe she'd take the chair. We don't know what goes on in the homes of everybody in West Virginia or any other place."

Ma's quiet a long while. I sit there listening to the crackle and hiss from inside our wood stove.

"I've an idea of something I might do," she says finally. "Judith keeps asking is there anything she can do for me, for keeping Ruthie here after school when she drives Rachel to her piano lesson. Well, there was a flyer on the bulletin board at Wallace's store about a weekly parenting class. It'll be over in the New Martinsville Library starting in January, folks getting together with a social worker to talk about being better parents. What if I told her I'd like to go, and could she drive me? I'll say now that we have children in middle school, we want to be raising them right. It said they offer child care if you have to bring a preschooler."

Dad thinks that over. "What if she offers to drop you off and pick you up later? If you're the only one who stays for the discussion?"

"It's a forty-minute drive to New Martinsville, Ray. I'd think she'd stay. But . . . well, if that happens, I'll just be a better parent," says Ma.

"It still doesn't involve the preacher," Dad tells her.

"No, but maybe it would help Judith stand up for herself and the girls," says Ma.

"Can't think of anything better," says Dad.

The next Sunday, as Dad is putting on his old work pants and shirt—his tool belt around his waist—I put on my oldest clothes too and find a warm cap and gloves from the box by the door.

When Dad sees me waiting after Ma and the girls have gone to church, he stops for a minute and sighs. "Marty, I'm not working on the new addition today," he tells me.

I say, "I know."

"I'll be over across the creek," he says.

"I'm ready," I tell him.

And then his face breaks into a smile. "C'mon, then," he says.

It's hard business, clearing land of all that burned-up stuff, and in five minutes, I'm sweating under my jacket. Most of the folks who lived across the creek have hired contractors to do part of the building for them. But some are doing the rebuilding themselves to save money, and anything we can do to clear the land, dig out the foundations, the more they'll save not paying someone else to do it.

We're working at Clay Fisher's house, digging all the debris out of the place used to be his garage, when Judd drives along in his pickup.

He stops to wave at me and Dad and sees the pile of charred wood and metal we've piled up alongside the road.

"You want that hauled away?" he calls. Wonder if he knows that Clay Fisher was one of the people saying Judd had set the fire.

Dad turns to Clay for an answer.

"It's not sittin' out there for decoration," Clay yells back, not even looking at Judd.

I see the way Judd stiffens up, way he used to look sometimes before he'd gun the motor and roar off. But then I see him take a breath, and he says, "Some folks want the metal sold to the junkyard. Just asking."

The other men stop their work and they all look at Clay.

"Uh . . . no, you can take the lot," Clay says. And when Judd gets out of the truck and starts piling the stuff in his pickup, I go over to help. And then, so does Clay.

Some of the church ladies come by around one o'clock bringing us fried chicken, coleslaw, and rolls, and we dive into that food like we haven't eaten for a week. Then we set to work again, and Judd's right there helping push a wheelbarrow and lift a cement block, shovel out a new trench, load his pickup for another run to the dump.

Near the end of the afternoon, Judd and I go on down to where his trailer used to be, and I help clear out his property. Most of his neighbors' burned houses been picked over, folks pulling out metal picture frames and medicine cabinets, eyeglasses and bedsprings . . . almost none of it any good, but it's all that's left after the fire.

But Judd hadn't done nothing yet. When his dogs ran off, he couldn't make up his mind to stay or leave. But now we pick over what the fire didn't get—not much—and at the end of the afternoon, Judd's ready to see it all go and start over.

He comes back to our house to use the shower, then drives all the way down to Middlebourne to visit his dog. And after dark sets in, we turn on those Christmas lights, and Dara Lynn talks Dad into driving us down the road to see if we can see them as far as the bend; then he drives us back and crosses the bridge, driving along Old Creek Road to see how far north a driver will see the lights. And when she's satisfied we got the most beautiful

Christmas decorations in the whole neighborhood—meaning she'd flunk the Christmas Spirit test if there was one—we head back home.

Fifteen days before Christmas, and I finish Rachel's biography. I don't say what kind of work her dad does. Don't mention her parents at all, just that the family had lived in a number of different places in West Virginia, two of them being Hinton and Weston, before they moved here.

Told what she'd said about how it feels to move to a new place, start all over again with everything, and how the person she likes most in the whole world is her little sister, Ruthie. How much she likes dance, would like to take interpretive dancing if she goes to college—the kind of dance that tells a story. At the end of the piece, I say that the most noticeable thing about Rachel Dawes is her smile, and that the question I'd most like to have asked her was what kind of story Rachel would tell if she ever became an interpretive dancer.

I let her read it before I turn it in. She smiles again when she reads that last line. Changes a couple things, where I don't have the facts right, and then I hand it in. I'm still working on my own autobiographical essay. Asked Rachel, does she want an extra copy of hers to take home, and she says no. But later, she comes by my locker to say yes, she'd like one to give her grandmother when they go there for Christmas.

We get our first real snowfall on Sunday. Becky wakes up that morning, looks out the window, and yells, "Is it Christmas?" Snow sure can make things look Christmas-pretty. For the first time I get Shiloh to walk across the bridge with me, and I wonder what it was that made the difference.

I can tell, what with Judd Travers staying with us, that Shiloh don't fear him as much as he used to. Maybe not much at all. Or maybe it was because the snow made the landscape look a lot different from what he remembered, covering up the things that brought back feelings he didn't ever want to have again. I look at the burned-out places that've now got a sparkly white blanket over them. The trees that stood scorched, their bark half-burned, all have an inch of snow covering their wounded branches.

We get us a normal snowfall here in West Virginia, we can deal with that okay. The trucks are out all night sprinkling salt, and plows get the highways ready. But if we have a really heavy snow—three feet, sometimes—not even Moses and the Israelites could get through some of the mountain passes. This one, though, we do just fine.

Dad tells Judd he's welcome to bring his sleeping bag inside, but he just laughs, says he's so used to the tent now that he maybe can't never sleep under a roof again.

Snow puts Doc Murphy in the Christmas mood, though. He says if I'll put up his Christmas tree, my bill will be paid off, and I'm glad to do it. He's got the artificial kind, the branches flocked with white, and I take it out of its box in his attic and set it up there in his living room.

Then I get the boxes of ornaments from a closet, and after Doc sees his last patient of the day, he closes his office door and sits down in his favorite chair.

"How 'bout if I put the hooks on and hand them up to you," he says.

"That'll work," I tell him, glad for the company.

"Now . . . this one was my wife's favorite," he says, holding up a little silver teapot with a sprig of holly painted on one side, and smiles. "We had a cat back then and had to put it up high enough that Molly couldn't swat at it with her paw."

I find the right branch for the teapot, and he's already handing me a little glass violin with a story to go along with it. I look at the boxes of ornaments lined up there on the couch and figure if there's a story to go along with each one, I'm like to be here till New Year's.

At one point, though, he gives me a red glass ball with a miniature snowman inside and tells me that one of his patients gave it to him years ago, then called him a month later. "Said he had something he wanted to talk over with me about a decision he had to make, and I told him I'd be glad to see him the next day. Next day comes, he never kept the appointment. Found out he moved away the following week. Always wondered what that decision was, and how it turned out," Doc says.

"I guess folks tell you a lot of secrets," I say, as I hook that glass ball to a branch near the window.

"Oh, I don't know I'd call them secrets, exactly. But when you're discussing your body, the conversation's going to be on the private side," says Doc.

I reach for another ornament and study it a minute before I hang it. "What if . . . you was to find out things going on in somebody's family that . . . don't break the law, exactly, but don't seem right neither."

"This would be . . . uh . . . let's say, a hypothetical family, I guess?" Doc asks.

Not sure what hypothetical means. And then Doc must figure I don't know too, because he adds, "An imaginary family?"

"Yeah," I say. "Just 'what if.'"

He shrugs. "Depends. Anybody getting hurt?"

175

I think about Ruthie having to sit with her feet in ice water, if that really happened. "Let's say no. Not physically, anyway."

"Hmmm. Well, if this family just does things a little differently and everybody's happy . . ."

"What if they're not happy?" I say. "The kids, anyway."

"Well, if they came to me . . . as their doctor . . . and they were being sexually abused or physically abused or psychologically tortured or something, I'd have to report it. That's the law."

I pick up the next ornament, a candy cane, and hang it on a branch.

"Nothing like that," I say. And then I get this awful feeling Doc thinks I'm talking about my own family. That Dad and Ma are mistreating us.

"Just that this family's new in the community, see, and . . . maybe the father's so strict—got punishments for the least little thing—and you're the only one who knows how much they cry." I reach for the next ornament before it's ready.

Doc takes his time finding a hook for it. Then he says, "Well, if I was just a friend of the family, I think I might try to find out who their doctor was and let him know. And then, if I was the doctor, I'd do my best to treat the whole family—find a good counselor who could help them out, if I wasn't able to do the job myself. And, of course, I'd be grateful to the person who let me know about it, because doctors can't always tell just by looking at a sore throat or an earache what other kinds of aches go on in a family."

"That's . . . good to know," I say. And I take the little ceramic angel and put her up near the top of the tree.

Last week of school before Christmas vacation. I come home on Wednesday, Shiloh at the bus stop to meet me, and when I get to the house, I find Dara Lynn and Becky and Ruthie sitting on the rug playing cards. One nice thing about Dara Lynn, she includes Becky a lot in her play, even when she brings Ruthie home with her. Somethin' strange about it, though—their fingers are doing the card dropping, but their eyes are on Ma and me. Becky's kneeling beside them holding Tangerine, face all serious. These girls are up to something, that's for sure. Wonder if they'd been trying to dress up my dog again before I got here.

"What you guys playing?" I ask as I put down my backpack and hang up my jacket.

Dara Lynn looks down at the cards like she don't even know. "Hearts," she says.

"No! It's Crazy Eights!" says Ruthie, and she gives Dara Lynn a look.

Ma's got her little portable sewing machine on the table, working on some red and green place mats, snowflake pattern.

"Ruthie here for dinner?" I ask as I check the refrigerator for something to eat.

"No, her mom took Rachel shopping, so she came home with Dara Lynn. Usually Judith calls me first, but I guess she forgot. Everybody's so busy getting ready for Christmas," Ma says.

I hold out a bowl of something yellow. "This vanilla pudding? Can I have it?"

"No, it's chicken gravy, Marty," Ma says, laughing. "You'll find some sliced ham in the bin below."

I get out crackers and the ham and take them to the other side of the table, then spread out my math homework. Every little thing I do, I got three pair of eyes on me.

"You guys want a snack?" I ask the girls. Three heads shake no. So I eat what's before me and work out the first two problems. When I look up again, Dara Lynn's slowly putting the cards back in the box and Ruthie's on her knees, head on the couch, holding her stomach.

"What's wrong?" I ask.

178

"Ruthie's got a tummy ache," says Becky, letting the cat go and crawling over to pat Ruthie on the back.

Ma stops the sewing machine and looks up. "Aren't you feeling well, Ruthie?" she asks.

"Just a stomach ache," says Dara Lynn quickly.

I get up to pour me a glass of milk, and I see the telephone dangling by its cord.

"Hey!" I say. "Who left the phone off the hook?"

Ma looks around. "For heaven's sake! Dara Lynn, did you leave it like that?"

Dara Lynn and Becky both snap to attention, but Ruthie stays buried in the couch.

"Maybe I bumped it accidentally," says Dara Lynn.

Ma stares at it. "No wonder I haven't heard from Judith." And then to Dara Lynn, "You've got to be more careful." But she studies the girls some more, then gets up and goes over to sit on the couch beside Ruthie.

"Sweetheart," Ma says, stroking her head. "Does your mom know you're here?"

Dara Lynn and Ruthie don't make a sound, but Becky shakes her head.

Ma looks directly at Dara Lynn. "Dara Lynn, did you leave that phone off the hook on purpose?"

Becky's nodding her head yes.

And suddenly Ruthie raises up and buries her head

179

in Ma's lap, and Dara Lynn says, "Mom, could Ruthie live here for a while?"

"*What?*" says Ma.

Ruthie's shoulders are shaking, and Ma forgets all about those place mats she was sewing.

The phone rings, and now all three girls are crying.

"Ruthie, did you come home with Dara Lynn without telling your mom?" asks Ma. Ruthie cries harder. I got me a whole drama going on right here in the living room and don't even have to buy a ticket.

"I'd better get that," says Ma, and slides Ruthie's head off her lap. I lift up the phone and hand it to Ma.

"Yes, Judith," she says, after listening a bit, "she's here. . . . Yes. . . . I know, your line was busy too."

Dara Lynn's eyes open wide, and Ma turns away.

"Oh, you know how forgetful the girls are when they get to talking. . . . Isn't that the truth! . . . Well, the driver must have misunderstood, though Dara Lynn could talk a chicken out of an egg. . . ."

Dara Lynn's mouth pops open.

"No, Ray's not here either, but couldn't you let Ruthie stay for dinner, and Ray will take her home later? . . . Oh . . . Oh, for goodness' sake . . . Of course, he's right here. . . ." And suddenly Ma's handing me the phone.

How did I get into this? I've only been home twenty minutes.

"Hello?" I say.

Mrs. Dawes's voice is either frantic or exasperated, I can't tell. "Marty, I don't know what's going on today, but neither of my daughters made it home. Was Rachel on the bus with you?"

My heart starts beating a little faster. "Yes, ma'am, she was," I say.

"Did she get off at our stop?"

I'm trying to remember. Only two people get off at the road where Rachel lives, and it's a five-minute walk to get to the Dawes's house from there. One or two houses and a field to pass by. Still, if Rachel got off there, she'd have been home way long before this.

"I think so," I say, but not real sure. "I think Jennie Harris gets off there too."

"I know. I've tried her number, but no one answers."

I'm trying to think of where she was sitting on the bus—where I was sitting. I was behind two of the guys on the basketball team, listening to them talk about a game.

"Well . . . ," says Mrs. Dawes. "I'll try another one of her friends. Jacob's making sick rounds this afternoon. I don't know when he'll be home. I'd come for Ruthie myself, but I want to stay near the phone in case Rachel calls. I appreciate you keeping Ruthie there till Jacob can pick her up."

Everybody's staring at me when I hang up the phone.

"She says Rachel didn't come home either," I tell Ma.

Ruthie is crying real hard now, a kind of choking crying, and Ma looks around the room. "Does *anybody* know what's going on?" she asks.

But Dara Lynn's still staring at Ma. "You told a lie!" she says.

Ma looks sheepish. "I . . . I guess I did. I didn't want to blame Ruthie!"

"But you blamed *me*!" Dara Lynn's downright triumphant. Caught her own ma in a lie.

"I'm sorry, Dara Lynn. I was flustered," says Ma. Then, "Does *any*one know where Rachel went?"

"Rachel ran away," says Becky.

fifteen

JUDD TRAVERS KNOCKS AT THE DOOR JUST THEN.

I open it for him. "Don't ask me to explain nothing," I say, as he looks around the room at the tear-streaked faces.

"I . . . uh . . . found one of your hens down by the road there," he says to Ma. "I put her back, but I think I see where they're getting out. If you've got some extra fencing, I'll see if I can fix it."

"Thanks, Judd, but right now we've got a missing girl, and I can't think straight," says Ma.

"And Ruthie's got a tummy ache," Becky tells him.

Judd studies Ruthie, head on the couch. "She need a doctor? Can I drive you somewhere?" he asks Ma.

"No, but Ruthie—she's the preacher's daughter—wasn't supposed to come here, and her sister Rachel didn't get home, and Ray's not home yet, and the preacher's out making his rounds, and Mrs. Dawes and I are going a little bit crazy."

Judd nods and starts to leave. Then turns around, hand still on the doorknob. "Rachel's the older girl, right?"

"Yes," says Ma.

"I seen a girl going in the side door of the church when I was on my way here. Didn't pay it all that much attention, and I wouldn't know if it was her or not. Eleven or twelve years old, maybe?"

Now Ma turns to the girls again, and you can tell by her face there's going to be no more guessing games. "Do *any* of you know where Rachel was going?"

All three heads shake in unison, even Becky's.

"How far is Rachel's bus stop from the church, Marty?" Ma asks. "Could she have walked it?"

"A mile, maybe."

"Judd, could you and Marty check that out? I don't want to get Judith's hopes up if Rachel's not there, but I don't know of anything going on at the church this afternoon. If she just wanted to get away, think things over, maybe she went there."

I agree it's possible, but knowing Rachel, seems to me that's about the last place she'd run to.

———

It's another twenty minutes to the church. No cars in the parking lot—been cleared of snow for over a week now. Front door's kept locked when there's nothin' going on, but side door's usually open during the day—somebody wants to come in, practice playing a hymn or just pray, they can.

Judd parks the pickup, and we open the side door and step into the little room next to the pulpit. No lights on, so when we go into the sanctuary, looks more like evening than afternoon.

Right away, though, I see that somebody's been here. Hymnbooks are scattered all around the platform in front—thrown, some of 'em, it looks like—and the pulpit itself is knocked over. I know it's not raccoons.

And then we hear a shuffling sound, and turn to see Rachel standing between the pews near the back. I think she sees Judd first, though, cause she gives a little gasp. Then she sees me.

"Hey, Rachel?" I call out.

She sits down hard and don't answer, her back straight as a rifle. When we get about five rows away from her, she says, "I'm *not* going home!"

I can tell that Judd's going to let me do the talking, seeing as how they never met.

"Okay," I say. "Didn't want to take you there. Just wanted to make sure you're all right. This here's Judd Travers."

She studies him curiously. Probably heard the same stories about him everyone else has heard. She don't say hello. Only, "How did you know where I was?"

"Judd saw you go in the church but didn't know you were missing. Just found out, and Ma asked us to ride here, make sure you were okay." I'm pushing it, I know, but I add, "Might could bring you a pillow and some supper, if you want."

Judd figures this is going to be a long conversation, so he sits down in a pew two rows in front of her, half-turned, with one arm slung along the back. Rachel don't answer.

Finally she says, "Does my dad know where I am?"

"I don't think so. We didn't even tell your ma."

"Good. I hope he worries his heart out, though I doubt it."

I sit down on the other side of the aisle, and we listen to a car go by on the road outside. When nobody talks for a while, Rachel says, "The only thing I worry about is Ruthie. They're probably giving her the third degree."

"Naw," I say. "She's at our house. She come home with Dara Lynn, and your ma's been looking for her."

"She's at *your* place?" Rachel asks, surprised.

"Yeah. Scared to go home without you."

Rachel lets out her breath. "She knew I was going to run away. I told her this morning, so she wouldn't think I'd been in an accident or something. I said not to tell anybody."

"She didn't. Not for a long while. But when your ma called . . . it's hard to keep that a secret when you're only seven," I say.

I can tell there's so much anger boiling up inside Rachel she can hardly hold back. Leaking out every which way. "I *wanted* to go to Ashley's house, but you can't take a different bus home without a note from your parents. And I'm *not* going home!" she says again. She stares down at her lap. "When I got off the bus this afternoon, I'd forgotten my mittens, and my hands were freezing. The only public building remotely close was the church, so I came here just to get warm."

Judd looks around the dim sanctuary. Only a couple of exit lights are lit. "Must be pretty strong to knock that pulpit over by yourself," he says.

"Wasn't so hard," says Rachel defiantly. She finds a hymnbook on the back of the seat in front of her. Must have missed that one. Picks it up and tosses it down the pew.

"*That's* what I think of my dad!" she says, and her voice trembles, she wants it to or not. "You can't *ever* please him, no matter what!" And then, after a minute or two, she asks, "Did you ever run away?"

Don't know who she's talking to, 'cause she don't look at either one of us.

But Judd surprises me when he's the one who answers. "Lots of times," he says. "Only I never had a place to go to, so always came home again, knowing a beating was waiting for me when I got there."

"Oh!" says Rachel, little quick breath.

"I was the youngest in my family," Judd says. "Three older brothers and one sister. One by one they all left, soon as they could. One took the car, one took my dad's shotgun and rifles, and the other two . . . I guess they took what money they could get their hands on. And there I was by myself with my dad. Ma had died when I was fourteen or so. Fifteen, maybe it was."

"You just . . . kept taking the beatings?" Rachel asks.

Strange they're carrying on a conversation without looking at each other. But it works.

"Oh, I had a plan, and that's the only thing kept me going," Judd tells her. "Friend of mine gives me his old rowboat. Moving away, don't want to take it with him. And since I got no car, no money, my plan was to fix up that rowboat, all the places it might leak, and get it down as far as Friendly, to the Ohio River, and that's the way I was going to clear out. Like that kid in the book . . . you know the one . . . Huck?"

"Yeah," I say. "Huckleberry Finn."

"That's the one. I got maps from the gas station, got my route all planned. . . ." Judd chuckles a little. "Going to take all the food in the refrigerator with me, all I can stow away, and when that's gone, I'll fish. You sure get some weird ideas when you're fifteen.

"And then," says Judd, "our house caught fire, and a week later my dad died of a heart attack." He shakes his head a little. "Not a single one of my brothers come back to bury him. My sister came to bring me some money, but Dad owned the piece of land we were living on, and nobody else wanted it, so it was turned over to me. I stayed, and finally bought my own trailer, and then some dogs."

"Wow," says Rachel. She looks at me, so I guess I'm supposed to say something.

"I never ran away, but I thought about it," I tell her. "It was when Ma discovered I was hiding a dog up in the woods. I begged her not to tell Dad, and got her to agree to wait till the next day at least. She only said yes when I promised I wouldn't run away with him."

Judd's looking at me funny, and then I realize that's a part of the Shiloh story he don't know.

"That was a dog you wanted to keep?" Rachel asks.

"Yeah," I say. "And . . . finally . . . they said I could." No need to tell the full story right now.

For a long while, none of us says anything. And then Rachel says, "So it looks like I'm just stuck, doesn't it?"

But Judd says, "Don't keep you from makin' plans. Only thing that kept me from bein' crazy while I was living at home was workin' on that rowboat. Planning it all out in my mind how I was going to make my escape. Dad would be in that house, drinkin', raving mad, I'd just go back in the woods there and do some more scraping, filling up holes in the rowboat."

"Too bad I don't have a rowboat," Rachel says, and her voice has a sting to it.

"Don't have to have a boat, girl. Your folks are probably planning to send you to college, aren't they? You can be out of the house then."

"That's six years off!" Rachel cries.

"Not too early to start collecting catalogs and applications and stuff, though," I tell her.

"My dad would see everything I get through the mail. He'd want to pick the college," says Rachel.

"Get them through the school counselor, then," I tell

her. I don't know a whole lot about the counselor, but I'd listened to her talk during orientation that first day of school. "Try to get a scholarship to the one you like best."

Judd's nodding his head. "It'll be your escape, same as the rowboat was for me. You can look through those catalogs or whatever and dream, and let me tell you, I had some big dreams. Just turned out I never needed to use 'em."

Nobody says anything for a while. I can see it's almost dark outside. Finally I tell Rachel, "Ruthie claims she has a stomach ache. You want to come back to my house? Maybe she'd feel better if she saw you."

Rachel thinks it over. "If we go straight to your house and not mine," she says.

"That's where I'm headed," says Judd. "But maybe we better put things to rights here before we go."

And Rachel starts picking up the hymnbooks.

We get home, and Judd says he's going to work on that chicken wire to make sure the hens don't get out again. So Rachel follows me into the house, and we're only in there about one minute before Dad gets home. He walks in to see Ruthie hugging Rachel and Ma saying, "Thank goodness!" And Becky and Dara Lynn begging Ma, can they stay for dinner?

When Ma says she needs to call Judith and tell her we've found Rachel, Rachel turns to her and says, "I don't want to go home!" And her voice trembles.

"It's because of Daddy," Ruthie puts in, watching her sister.

"And Christmas and *everything*!" Rachel says, with a catch in her throat. And then, after being like a soldier all this time, she sits down and starts to cry.

Dad slowly hangs up his jacket, like if he makes the slightest noise we're all going to explode. Since he came in after the show begun, he don't have any idea what's going on, but he don't want to be the one to light the match.

"Yesterday was Dad's birthday," Rachel says through her tears. She's wiping her eyes with the back of one hand and trying to keep her voice steady. "Ruthie and I . . . have been saving up our money . . . for a present . . . and Christmas too . . . and last night we gave him . . ." Her voice wavers.

"A box of handkerchiefs," says Ruthie, trying to help out. "And he told Rachel to take them back."

"What?" says Ma, can't believe what she's hearing.

Rachel's in control of herself again, and I can hear the anger coming through. "He said he'd been watching us in church . . . and how . . . for the past two Sundays we hadn't put anything in the offering plate . . . and how Jesus had to come before anything else. So he wanted me to get a refund and—"

"And give it to Jesus for his birthday," Ruthie finishes.

Dad gives a low whistle.

Ma says, "Girls, I'm so sorry. I think he means well, really. . . ."

"He means just what he says, that he doesn't want the stupid old handkerchiefs," says Rachel.

"What did you do with them?" Ruthie asks her.

Rachel looks around, almost afraid to tell us. "I threw them in the creek."

I get the box of tissues from the kitchen counter and put it between the girls on the couch. Dara Lynn's got this grim look on her face, like we got to let them stay for dinner, while Becky's crying just 'cause Ruthie and Rachel are crying again, and Shiloh's gone over to sit next to her.

Dad looks completely confused. Ma turns to him. "Ray, Ruthie came home from school with Dara Lynn without her mom's permission, and Rachel ran away . . . as far as the church. Judd saw her go in, so he and Marty went after her and brought her here. Judith's frantic about Rachel. I told her Ruthie was here."

Dad's had a hard day delivering all the Christmas cards and packages—five times as much mail as usual this time every year, he tells us, and I know he wants to sit down and get his shoes off more than anything, but he says, "I'd be angry too, Rachel; indeed I would. But we still have to let your parents know where you are."

Rachel don't fight it. She knows she's got to go home. Got Ruthie to think about now, and at least she had the chance to dump those handkerchiefs in the creek. Creek sure getting a lot of business from her, I'm thinking.

Ma picks up the phone and calls Mrs. Dawes. "Judith, we've got Rachel," she says. "Yes . . . she's fine. Upset, but okay. Judd Travers saw her go into the church, so he and Marty brought her back in Judd's pickup." That must have been some surprise to Mrs. Dawes, 'cause Ma's saying, "Yes . . . Judd Travers . . . That's right. He's been so helpful."

But when she hangs up, she says, "I'm afraid you can't stay for dinner, girls. Your dad just got home, and he was already on his way to pick up Ruthie. He'll be here in a few minutes. We'd love to have you another time."

Rachel stiffens, and Ruthie bends over again, arms over her stomach. We sit around waiting. Dara Lynn brings out Tangerine and tries to amuse the girls by dragging a piece of crinkle ribbon across the rug to watch the cat pounce. But it don't seem as funny as it usually does.

I hear a car coming up the lane and look out the side window.

"Preacher's here," I say.

Ma brings out Ruthie's jacket, and Ruthie suddenly throws her arms around Ma's waist, won't let go, and Becky's started sucking her thumb. Haven't seen her do that in a long time.

Shiloh's barking out on the porch. He don't recognize the preacher.

Dad opens the door before the girls' daddy has a chance to knock.

"Would you like to come in, Pastor Dawes?" he says. "Guess there was a little mix-up. It happens."

But the preacher just stands at the doorway, looking in. "Rachel's here too?"

"Yes, they're both safe and sound," Ma says, trying to be cheerful, nudging Ruthie toward the door.

Rachel won't even look at her father. Stares straight ahead.

"Come on, Ruthie," the preacher says.

Ma has to loosen Ruthie's fingers on her shirt, and the girl takes her dad's hand, sniveling.

"That's enough," Preacher says to Ruthie. And then to Ma, "Thank you for taking care of her."

"Don't be too hard on her," Ma pleads, and I squeeze by them onto the porch to hold Shiloh back.

Preacher turns to leave, but he don't know what all his girls have told us, and he's got something to say: "I go by the Bible: 'Children, obey your parents in all things, for this is well pleasing unto the Lord.'"

Dad walks down the steps beside him. "Yes, I know the verse and the one after: 'Fathers, provoke not your children to anger, lest they be discouraged.'" And as they reach the car, Dad says real gentle, "Pastor, you've got two daughters who want to love their father. Don't make it so hard for 'em."

Preacher don't answer. He opens the back door for Ruthie, throws her pink backpack in beside her, then opens the front passenger-side door for Rachel. But she slams it and crawls in the back beside Ruthie. Preacher goes around to the driver's side. "Good night," he says. And they drive off into the dark.

sixteen

EVERYBODY'S CRYING ALL OVER AGAIN WHEN WE COME back in.

"That was the hardest thing I ever had to do, Ray," Ma says. "Ruthie's such a little thing, and she was shaking like a leaf."

"We had no choice, Lou," says Dad, and guides her over to the couch. The rest of us find places to sit. Not a one of us leaving this room, 'cause we all had some part in the situation.

We talk it out a little more, and then Ma says, "You can cripple a child without ever laying a hand on her. But he's crippled himself more. While we were workin' on that Thanksgiving dinner, Judith told me that Jacob's bringing up those girls the same way he was raised.

Takes the half of the Bible talking about sin and guilt and punishment, and forgets the verses about love and forgiveness."

Dad nods. "Doesn't know a better way," he says.

"I keep hoping I can reach him through Judith, but I think she's a little afraid of him too." Ma wipes her eyes. "She said she'd been trying for a half hour to reach us when Ruthie didn't get off the bus, but our line was always busy." She glances over at Dara Lynn.

Dara Lynn don't even try to sound sorry. "And you lied!"

"Yes . . ."

Dad looks at Ma.

"I told Judith that the girls just got talking on the bus and missed Ruthie's stop, and that's not the way it happened," Ma explains.

"You said I could talk a chicken out of an egg!" Dara Lynn corrects her.

"She *what*?" says Dad, a trace of a smile on his face.

"I'm sorry, Dara Lynn. I guess I didn't want to pile any more trouble on Ruthie. But I forgive you for bringing her home and lying to me about it."

"Then I forgive you for lying to Ruthie's ma," says Dara Lynn, satisfied she won her case. Boy, anybody take Dara Lynn to court, I sure pity the judge.

"Sometimes," Dad says, "we hardly know what we're going to do about a situation till we're in it."

Is he remembering how he made me give Shiloh back to Judd Travers that first time Shiloh ran away? Remembering how Shiloh was shaking and trembly, and as soon as he got his feet on the ground, Judd gave him a kick? Think he is, 'cause later, when we sit down to eat, just the way he squeezes my shoulder . . .

Next day Dara Lynn comes home and says Ruthie's dad didn't punish them this time. He told Rachel perhaps he was a little hasty in telling her to get a refund on those handkerchiefs, that they were a gift from the girls and he should have thanked them. And Rachel tells him if he wants his handkerchiefs back, he can go look in the creek. Nothing the preacher can do about that.

Next morning Dad's taking the day off at the post office, and he's got the ax and the sled ready. Time to go chop us down a Christmas tree.

Our property's loaded with fir trees. Everybody's got a different idea of where to look, and Becky is all bundled up with scarves and mittens. She don't care how far we go, long as she's the one on the sled.

"Let's don't get any tree taller than my head," Dad

tells us. "Once it's on the stand with an angel on top, we don't want it scratching the ceiling."

We decide on a balsam pine and stand to one side while Dad chops it down.

Shiloh goes with us. I'm wishing there was a way I could teach him to stay on our property. Most of our seventy acres are hilly and rocky—can't do much of anything with them, but Dad likes the idea of space on all sides. Plenty of land for a dog to explore.

If I could just tell Shiloh never to cross the road, and that the highway the other side of our woods is off-limits. Tell him that when you get as high as the overlook, you're on somebody else's land. You can teach a dog a lot, but he don't understand everything.

Once we get the pine tree chopped down, we load it onto the sled and head back.

Dara Lynn starts singing "Jingle Bells," and the rest of us join in. That's one thing everybody in our family can do—sing.

It's taking longer to get that Christmas tree through the woods than it took us to get up there. First off, the sled's too small, and the tree keeps falling off. Little blue sled I had since I was five years old. Becky's getting cold, now that she has to walk in the snow, and she and Ma and Dara Lynn go on ahead. Dad and I finally reach the open stretch back of our house—all downhill from here.

And as we're pulling at that rope, Dad says, "Marty, have you ever been afraid of me?"

I can tell that the preacher and his daughters are still on his mind.

"No," I say, "but . . . sometimes . . . I been afraid of what you might say."

"Well, that's the same thing, isn't it? I just don't like the thought of you or the girls ever being scared of their pa."

"I was afraid you wouldn't let me keep Shiloh last year," I tell him. "Guess that's the one time I can think of."

I glance over at him and he nods, so I keep talking.

"That night . . . the night the German shepherd come and broke into that pen I'd built for Shiloh—and you found him and put him in the car—that's the most scared I've ever been. Of what you might do. If you had driven Shiloh over to Judd's that night, his leg all torn up, and left him there, I . . . I don't know what *I* would have done."

"Guess I couldn't stand to see a dog in pain any more than you could," Dad says.

"Well . . . I've finally worked off my bill to Doc Murphy," I tell him.

Dad looks over. "Really? Good job, Marty! You've worked for him a whole year. He ever tell you what he charged for all that stitching up and those antibiotics?"

"No. I just took his word for it. But he says we're fair and square."

"I'm glad to hear it. A person who keeps to his side of a bargain is a man you can trust."

"And I've never lied to you since then, neither."

Dad's big arm reaches over and gives me a hug. "I believe that, Marty," he says. "You've grown up a whole lot this past year. And I hope there's never anything you feel you can't talk to me about."

"Well . . . I got a lot of *whys*," I tell him.

"Questions? About . . . ?" He waits.

"Just stuff," I tell him. "About people . . . dogs . . . God . . ."

"Don't ever stop asking questions in this life," he says. "I won't have all the answers, but we'll have us some good conversations." He looks over at me. "Something on your mind right now?"

"Naw," I say, and smile back. "But when I get a good one, I'll let you know."

Mr. Kelly says if we don't want anybody but him to read our autobiographical essay, to write *Private* in the upper right-hand corner. Fred Hilt asks, if we don't want *anybody* to read it, can we just turn in two blank sheets of paper? Everyone laughs.

"Just try it," says Mr. Kelly, and we laugh some more.

I've been writing mine slowly, a little at a time, and I turn it in a few days before Christmas vacation.

The Friend I Used to Hate (private)
by Marty Preston

There were a dozen reasons I hated Judd Travers, but the biggest was the way he treated his dogs. Some folks take pleasure in being cruel, and he was one of them.

But the time he bought himself a new beagle hunting dog, and that dog run away, come to me, it changed my life, and changed Judd too. Because neither Judd or me either one knew that someday Shiloh was going to save Judd's life, and later on, Judd was going to save his.

What I learned in the meantime is that there's a whole lot to think about between right, on one side, and wrong, on the other. . . .

Mr. Kelly asks if anybody wants to read his paper to the class before we turn them in, and David Howard reads his. He writes how his family was visiting relatives in Wisconsin once when he was six years old—all the cousins splashing around in the lake—and he steps in this hole and goes under. Don't know how to swim. He remembers green bubbles floating up from his nose and mouth, and finally he's rescued by a cousin. And because of that he takes swim lessons, and gets up to Shark, and even gets a diving certificate.

Laura Herndon writes a really funny essay. She titles it "My First Rodeo," and says when she was four, her dad took the kids to a carnival. Only thing she was big enough to go on was the pony ride. A teenage boy lifts her onto a pony and starts around the ring, but he gets to flirting with one of the girls leading another pony, and somehow Laura starts sliding to one side of the saddle, a little at a time. When the boy finally looks around, he sees just a foot up there on the saddle, Laura dangling down the other side of the horse, hanging on to the mane.

We really laugh about that one. We spend the rest of the class period talking about perspective. Mr. Kelly tells us to imagine how our essays would have been written different if we could have wrote them back when they happened. David Howard said he would have still been so scared his hand would be shaking. But his essay was about how his fear got him to learn to do something important he might not have done if it hadn't happened.

Laura says if she had written her essay back then, it would have been almost too embarrassing to write about. But now it's funny.

I know that if I had written an essay about Judd Travers when I had to return Shiloh to him that first time, it would have been pure hate. H-A-T-E. Can't say it's love now—more like . . . understanding? Respect, maybe, for how a man can change.

Christmas falls on a Tuesday this year, so Friday's our last day of school till after New Year's. Our house sure has the holiday spirit. First off, coming up the lane from the school bus, I can smell the wood smoke coming out of our potbellied stove in the living room. It's snowed again, just enough to cover the ugly brown that was beginning to show up on old drifts along the road. Then, when I open the door, I smell the last batch of cookies Ma's baked to give away. And finally, if I go into the living room and get up close to the tree, I can smell the fresh scent of a balsam pine. A whole lot better than the fake spray they're selling at the dollar store, with a recording that every ten seconds says, "Balsam pine—it smells so fine."

Saturday, Dara Lynn and Becky spend the morning wrapping up their presents for the family, telling Ma and me not to look. Guess a person can't have too many macaroni necklaces or red-and-green pot holders made out of loops. That afternoon they go off to a birthday party at a neighbor's down the road, and I take Shiloh for a hike, using the long leash Dr. Collins give me for helping out so much during the year. This way Shiloh can trot off into the bushes and sniff to his heart's content, but can't never go far enough I can't rein him back to me when it's time to move on.

Now he's plumb tuckered out, stretched out there on the rag rug in front of the stove, so when Ma asks me to go along with her and deliver all the Christmas cookies she's baked, I'm glad to do it. She's made trays out of the lids of boxes, each one covered every inch with Christmas wrapping paper to look all fancy, with a card on top. Every tray's filled with the same cookies she makes each year: chocolate drops, almond crescents, butterscotch swirls, pecan bars. . . . Just saying the names make my tongue ache.

One tray goes to the preacher's; one to Mrs. Sweeney, who comes over sometimes to take care of Becky when

Ma gets a ride to town; Mr. and Mrs. Wallace at the store for putting our groceries on charge, they get one; another goes to Doc Murphy; and Ma always has a few more trays for any folks need cheering up.

Mrs. Sweeney, in fact, is so eager for those cookies that she tells Ma we can use their car to make deliveries. Then we don't have to wait till Dad's off on Sunday to use the Jeep. She drives her car over, and we make our first stop at her place.

"I can taste these cookies just by looking at them," she says as she gets out, holding the tray Ma made for her. "You folks take your time. I'm glad to help."

I slide back into the Sweeneys' car while Ma checks her list, and we're off to the Daweses' house next. Preacher's car is gone, so Ma steers the car right up the driveway. I take a tray from the backseat, go up the steps, and ring the bell.

Mrs. Dawes opens the door, and I can tell I come at a bad time, 'cause she looks even more tired than usual, and Ruthie is standing next to her, tears on her face. That girl ever stop crying? I wonder.

"Well, for goodness' sake, Marty, how nice!" Mrs. Dawes says, looking at the cookies there beneath the plastic wrap. "Please come in."

The wind's blowing right hard, so I'm glad to step

out of it for just a minute, and don't want to drop the tray.

"Don't tell me your mother baked all these herself!" she says.

"Yes, ma'am. She just wanted your family to have some," I say.

Ruthie's on tiptoe, looking at the cookies, but it don't stop the tears. Mrs. Dawes puts one hand on her head.

"Ruthie's so disappointed that—"

Suddenly Ma's at the door, and Mrs. Dawes opens it for her.

"Hi, Judith. Marty's helping me with deliveries this year, and your card just blew off the box. I chased it across the lawn," Ma says, laughing, and hands it to her. Then she sees Ruthie. "Oh, sweetheart! Why the tears?" she asks.

"Ruthie's disappointed because we can't go to her grandmother's for Christmas," Mrs. Dawes says. "This is something the girls really look forward to each year, but my mom just came down with the flu that's going around Parkersburg, so we've had to cancel our plans."

And now Ruthie's bawling all over again, and I see Rachel standing back in the hall.

And in two shakes, Ma says, "Then you're coming to

our house for Christmas dinner. That's all there is to it. We'd be delighted to have you, really!"

I stare at Mom.

Ruthie's face goes from sad to celebration in three seconds flat.

Mrs. Dawes looks all flustered. "Oh, Lou. I—I don't know—"

"Oh, Mommy, can't we go?" Ruthie begs, tugging at her arm.

"I just—Jacob's not here, and—"

"Judith, you know he has the day off already. Please do this for your girls," Ma says. Then she sees Rachel back by the stairs and says, "Rachel, wouldn't you like to come?"

Mrs. Dawes turns around. "Would you like that, Rachel?"

And Rachel gives her shy little smile. "Yes," she says.

Mrs. Dawes turns back. "All right, then. And thank you so much for the cookies. They look delicious."

"One o'clock, Christmas Day," Ma says. "We're casual. And of course we'll see you at the Christmas Eve service."

When we're back in the car, Ma says, "I can't believe I got her to say yes. Did you see the look on Ruthie's face when I invited them? You know the girls want to come."

"Ma . . . ," I say.

"And I think Rachel would enjoy it, don't you?"

"Ma," I say again. "Did you remember Judd Travers will be there too?"

And suddenly Ma gets that blank look on her face, and her hands go limp on the steering wheel. But she recovers and starts the engine. "Marty," she says, "we'll deal with it."

seventeen

As we head to Doc Murphy's, Ma and I are trying to remember all the different jobs I did for him this past year to pay him for stitching up Shiloh. I washed his windows, dug up an old fence and filled the postholes, weeded his garden, scrubbed his kitchen floor, cleaned out his garage, and finally put up his Christmas tree.

He's so glad to see those cookies that he slips a finger under the plastic wrap and slides one out that very minute, taking a bite of the butterscotch swirl.

"Tell your mom they get better every year," he says. And then, "Got something for you." Goes to his desk and comes back with an envelope. "Here you go."

I wish him a Merry Christmas and get in the car. While Ma's driving on to the next house, I open the envelope. Then I choke.

"Ma!" I cry out.

She almost slams on the brakes. "Marty!" she says. Sounds like we're just getting introduced.

I am staring at a check for five hundred dollars! Then I read the note out loud:

Marty: For a year I've watched you work off your debt to me. You never complained. Never asked how much longer you'd have to work, or said you'd expected it to be paid off by now, though you must have been thinking it. You have the qualities to become a good veterinarian, and if that's what you decide to do with your life, I hope this check will be the start of your college fund. Doc Murphy

Ma turns the car around, drives back up the road a piece, pulls in the driveway, and invites Doc to Christmas dinner.

Our happiness carries right over into supper, and even though Dad's bone-tired from delivering Christmas mail, he's feeling pretty proud of me. Proud of his whole family, right then. That's the way happiness is, you know. Contagious. Dara Lynn and Becky got the giggles, and Ma's so happy about getting her cookies delivered, and about that check, that when she realizes she had some stewed tomatoes on the stove top and forgot to serve them, she just laughs and says we'll eat them along with the cookies, and sets 'em both on the table. Shiloh makes his way from one of us to the other. Figures he might as well get in on the celebration, we got any crumbs to spare.

Since we're all going to church Monday night, Christmas Eve, Dad stays home from service the next day and heads over across the creek to help put up the frame of a new house for one that burned down. Belonged to the Keegans, a young couple expecting a new baby, their second child, in February. Judd goes over with him, and Sunday afternoon a number of men from church arrive in their work clothes, including Brother Hatch, everybody wanting to help this family that probably needs a place to go more than anyone.

I'm there too, doing whatever anybody needs— pound a board in place, look for a different kind of pliers, pour somebody a cup of coffee, lift a concrete block. Couple women arrive in the afternoon with ham sandwiches and apples and more of Ma's cookies. Nice to see Judd working right alongside the rest. Never had no mechanical training, but they say he picks up the work fast at Whelan's Garage, and he seems to know the basics of building a house.

I'm feeling real good about being there with all these men, helping build a new home for a new baby. Being treated like a man too—handed a cup of coffee just like everybody else.

We work until it's getting so dark we can't see much, and my hands are stiff from the cold, even though I got work gloves on. So finally we all pack up our tools and cover the unused lumber, everybody in a good mood, Christmas just two days away. Dad's whistling "O Come All Ye Faithful," and when Brother Hatch hears it, he starts to sing.

And then, wouldn't you know it, another voice joins in, and then another, and here's this pack of tired men, singing together in the frosty air, smiling at one another as first one, then another, climbs in his car and drives away.

Next morning, Christmas Eve day, Ma's got a lot to do in the kitchen, and I know I can help most by keeping the girls from bothering her, so I agree to play Monopoly with Dara Lynn. We let Becky be the banker. We tell her how much to pay out and how much to collect, and meanwhile she arranges all the extra houses and hotels in patterns off the board and has her own little game going on the side. Ma gives me a grateful look as she rolls out the crust for a pie.

In the afternoon, she takes index cards with the names of all our guests on them, and asks Becky and Dara Lynn to draw little Christmas decorations on the sides with green and red felt-tip pens, just so I can have a break. I put the Monopoly game away, and the second I get my jacket from the closet, Shiloh's up and ready for his hike. Don't think he cares all that much for the leash, but he can go pretty far on it, and sometimes I think he forgets it's there.

We walk down to the bridge, and this time, just like the last, Shiloh trots on across. Guess he's forgiven Judd for all the old meanness. I'm wondering how in the world Shiloh was able to track Judd's white dog and bring him back, unless maybe he could smell Judd's scent on him somehow and figured that dog should be out in our tent too. Wonder if he ran into any of those raccoons along the way.

If there were Ten Commandments for Dogs, I know what the first three would be: thou shalt be loyal, thou shalt be kind, and thou shalt be brave.

When I get back, I help Ma in the kitchen—peel potatoes and onions and chop up cranberries. We're all hoping Dad will be home in time to go to the Christmas Eve service. Last year he didn't get back from the post office till eight at night. We know he'll be tired no matter what.

But this time he's home by six, and we all of us go to church. Ma asks me to help the girls hang up their stockings before we leave, because it will be past Becky's bedtime when we get home, and she's grumpy when she's tired.

Dara Lynn won't do it unless I do it too, so I find me a clean tube sock with red and blue stripes at the top. Dara Lynn first comes out with a kneesock, biggest sock she can find, but I tell the girls that Santa knows that Ma's trying to keep things simple this year—all our extra money going to the new addition—so he'll do his part by leaving only a little. I tell them to find their prettiest sock, not the biggest, and soon we got three socks hanging in weird places in the living room, on account of we don't have any fireplace. One sock's on a drawer handle, one's on a lamp knob, and I got mine caught between the Bible and *Favorite Bedtime Stories* in the bookcase.

We ooh and aah at all the houses lit up along the

way as we drive to church. And when we get inside the sanctuary, it's got candles at the windows and red and white flowers on both sides of the pulpit. Becky loves that we sing songs she knows—"Away in a Manger" and "O Little Town of Bethlehem"—but I can see by her lips that when she don't know all the words, she makes them up.

Preacher Dawes has put aside sin and blasphemy this time; he reads the Christmas story from the book of Luke, about Mary and Joseph being turned away at the inn. And then he wonders how many of us would recognize Jesus and take him in if he came today.

After the service, someone turns out the lights, so all we've got is candlelight, and Brother Hatch leads us in "Silent Night." When we sing the last verse, he tells us, we should sing it real soft and make our way out to our cars.

I like that. We're singing as we go, and the preacher's at the door, just smiling and nodding as we pass by. When the last verse is finished, Mrs. Maxwell plays it again to make sure everybody has a chance to sing all the way out to the parking lot. I think about the men singing as they went to their cars the day before—the good feeling I had then and the good feeling I got now. And I'm thinking that my own idea of what religion should be is something that brings people together, don't separate 'em.

We talk about the sermon on the drive home, Christmas lights burning in the houses all along the road. Dad asks us would we recognize Jesus, and I say it depends. If a woman riding a donkey came up to our house wanting a place to sleep, I think we'd pay attention, Jesus or not. Figure the whole neighborhood would be out just to see the donkey.

"*I* wouldn't turn them away," says Becky. "Jesus could sleep in my bed and I'd sleep with Dara Lynn."

"Some people believe that there's a little bit of Jesus in every one of us, and we just don't recognize it," says Ma.

I think about that, and about the essay I wrote for Mr. Kelly. Maybe I was trying to say something like that. Anyway, Mr. Kelly gave me a good mark. Along the side he wrote, *Excellent insight here, Marty. Check out the mistakes in grammar. But I very much enjoyed your essay. Well done.*

Christmas morning. We're allowed to look in our stockings the minute we get up, but Ma's got a rule: we don't eat any candy until we have breakfast. She don't want it in our stomachs without some scrambled eggs to land on.

Becky's squealing about a tiny little doll made out

of cork and calico that I'm sure Ma made just for her, with a candy cane, a rubber frog for the bathtub, and some chocolates in red and green foil. Dara Lynn's got a tiny calico purse and a harmonica, and I got a knit cap and a dog whistle, supposed to be so high-pitched only dogs can hear it. Dara Lynn carries on about how Santa knows just what we want, and then she puts a big red bow on the back of Shiloh's collar. Looks like a hair ribbon behind his ear.

"Get that thing off my dog!" I tell her.

"Oh, it's Christmas, Marty," she says, and I let it stay as long as Shiloh will put up with it. Her cat has one too—a green one—that stays on for about three seconds; all Tangerine cares about is the end of the couch closest to our potbellied stove.

After we've eaten our scrambled eggs and sausage and honey toast, we carry our dishes to the sink and gather over by the Christmas tree. Several packages been added to the ones I put there the day before.

We open the presents the girls made first—a red-and-green macaroni necklace for Ma and bracelets for Dad and me, and we put 'em around our necks or on our wrists, and say "Just what we need to look Christmassy," and Dara Lynn points out we each got a red-and-green pot holder to go with it, and we exclaim some more.

After that, everyone opens their gifts from me—the free things I got from the animal clinic. Since all anybody got so far was macaroni necklaces, my gifts don't look so cheap, and they like them, every single one. Dad's happy the key chain flashlight gives off more light than you would think, and Ma says she'll hang up that dish towel for everybody to see when they come to dinner.

Even though Ma's gift from Dad was to be the icicle lights, he's got a little box for her under the tree with a tiny perfume sample the stores were giving out, and Ma's made a shirt for him that she sewed herself on the machine—a red-and-black flannel shirt. He takes off the one he's wearing and puts it right on, ready for company.

'Course, Dara Lynn and Becky can't wait to get to the bigger presents. Becky gets two, because hers are smaller, and a four-year-old always thinks that a big present is the best. In one box she got a stuffed pelican, you can store secrets in its pouch, and in the bigger one she got a microscope set for little kids, and I promise that as soon as all the presents are opened, I'll show her what to do with it.

I think she's disappointed, 'cause it don't look like anything she'd choose right off, but she's got her nose in Dara Lynn's wrapping paper, and in that box is a pair of knee-high boots with white fur around the top.

"Ma, it's the exact same thing that Corine has, and it's just what I wanted most of all in the whole world!" Dara Lynn cries.

And then I open the biggest box of all from Ma and Dad, and think how puny my gifts were compared to what they bought for us.

"Handle it gently, Marty," Ma says. And when I get the last of the tissue paper off, I lift out a lampshade that's got the map of the world on it, and then the desk lamp itself, with a heavy white base. I stand it upright and put the shade on top, and when I get a bulb in the socket, plug it in and turn it on, the shade's like a lighted map, and I can turn it around without the lamp turning. Not only that, but I discover that the base itself is a radio.

"For your room, when you move into it," Dad says.

"Man!" I keep saying. "Man, this is really great!" I can't wait to show it to David Howard. "Thank you." And I feel sort of cheap, I didn't pay a cent for the gifts I gave them. Then I think, well, I worked for them, so that's the same thing, I guess.

Becky's tearing up 'cause she got a present she don't know how to use, so we set the microscope up for her on the coffee table. Show her the slides that come with it—what a spider looks like flattened out and enlarged; a bee's leg; a leaf . . .

Dara Lynn wants to try it next. "You can try on my boots if I can have the microscope for a while," she says to Becky.

So Becky puts her feet in the boots—come clear up to the tops of her thighs—and she goes clomping around, happy as a clam, while Dara Lynn's putting all sorts of weird things under the microscope—a hair off Shiloh, a piece of fingernail, a dead fly from off the windowsill— and the girls are squealing and carrying on how nasty things look when they're bigger.

Suddenly Dara Lynn looks at me and says, "I forgot!"

She ducks back in her bedroom and comes out with another present for me. It's sort of flat, about a foot square.

"What's this?" I say.

"I was afraid it would get broken if I put it under the tree," she says. "Go ahead. Open it up."

"Wow," I say, and now I feel twice as bad for just giving her a little rubber mouse. "Wonder what it could be?"

This time it appears not even Becky knows, 'cause she's got one hand on my shoulder, face close to the wrapping paper.

I guess I've opened it facedown. Looks to be a piece of cardboard with a rope handle at the top. I turn it over. Glued to the cardboard are short pieces of green macaroni, and they spell out the words DO NOT DISTURB.

I look at Dara Lynn, but she's all smiles.

"To hang on the door of your room," she tells me.

An hour later I hear Judd dropping wood on our front porch. Dad let him use our hatchet, and he chopped up a lot of deadwood on our property. I'm wondering how Ma is going to tell him that she's invited the Daweses to Christmas dinner.

Judd knocks and comes in with an armload of kindling that's just the right size for our stove. He's stacking it, and I'm listening with both ears as Dad moves over to him and says in a low voice, "Judd, I got a favor to ask. When we found out that Pastor Dawes and his family couldn't go to the grandmother's house for Christmas on account of her having the flu, Lou invited them to come here."

I can see Judd's back stiffen and he stands there straight, a piece of wood in one hand, the stove door open. But Dad goes on, "Now, I don't always see eye to eye with the preacher, and I'd like you to sit down at my end of the table, and if you see I've started in on a subject that's getting under his collar, will you give my foot a nudge? I'm trying to keep this a happy dinner for the kids."

Judd bends down and feeds the wood to the fire. Don't say anything for a few seconds, and finally he says, "Yeah, if I don't say something first. You may have to nudge my whole leg to get me to stop."

"Deal," says Dad. "I think we can do it."

Talk about smooth.

eighteen

MA'S GOT CAROLS PLAYING ON THE RADIO, AND WE'RE waiting for Aunt Hettie to get here from Clarksburg.

I let Shiloh out to do his business and run around a little before company arrives, but after ten minutes I go whistle to call him back in. Can see the tip of his tail where he's moving around by the shadberry bush, so I whistle again. Finally he trots across the lawn and up onto the porch.

Takes me about two seconds to see that he's been rolling in fresh deer poop.

"Shiloh!" I yell, and yank him by his collar, a little more roughly than I should, and I feel bad I do that on Christmas day.

But I feel even worse that his breath smells all poopy too.

"Ma, he's been in deer poop again," I call.

"Oh, Shiloh!" says Ma, in disappointment.

You can love a dog and hate the mess, I've discovered.

It's too cold to bathe Shiloh outdoors, so the only thing to do is put him in the shower.

"Anybody want to use the bathroom, do it quick, 'cause I got to bathe this creature," I call out, and both girls take a turn.

Then I pull Shiloh into the bathroom, close the door, take off my shirt, and turn the water on. A minute later I know I should have put on a bathing suit, 'cause I'm practically in there with him.

"You miserable mutt," I say as I lather him up.

"You stinkin' hound," I tell him as I run my fingers through his coat, and pieces of poop fall off and dissolve over the drain.

"You freakin' numbskull," I growl as I spray him from nose to rump.

Finally I turn off the water and towel him dry. Going to have to give him a breath mint or something before the company gets here, but meanwhile I try to avoid his big brown eyes looking up at me.

"Why do I love you so much?" I ask him.

I bend down to wipe his paws, and he licks my cheek.

"Why is it you do these weird things and I forgive

you? Even though I know you'll go do it all over again?"
I say.

He licks the other cheek.

"Even if I build a fence, no guarantee you won't get
out of it. What you gonna do when I go off to veteri-
nary school, huh?"

My voice must be getting softer and gentler, because
all at once he turns himself around and around—doing
his little "happy dance," like he knows we're friends
again. His white coat with the big brown spots is all
fluffy and clean, and if only there was such a thing as
doggie mouthwash, he'd be ready to greet the guests.

Aunt Hettie pulls in about twelve. She says it was snow-
ing in Clarksburg when she left. I look out and sure
enough, snowflakes are coming down slow, not a one of
them in a hurry. We already got six inches of snow that's
stayed since our last snowfall. We tell Judd his tent's
likely to become an igloo.

"I smell turkey!" Hettie says, coming in the kitchen
door, a bag on each arm. Looks to be mostly food,
though. Don't see any gift wrap peeking out the top.

"Merry Christmas, Aunt Hettie," I say. She's Dad's
sister, but she's not that tall. Her hug's big, though, and
she swoops up each one of us in her arms. Even Shiloh

stands there, tail wagging, waiting his turn for a pat on the head.

"Look what I made for you!" Becky says, holding up a macaroni necklace, pieces of pink- and green- and orange-colored pasta on a string.

"What's this, precious?" Hettie says, and then, without missing a beat, "Now isn't this the prettiest!" and she slides it right on over her head, macaroni hanging down the front of her jacket.

Then she turns to us and says, "I decided on one big present for the five of you this year, and I need somebody to help me get it out of my station wagon."

Can't for the life of me think what that could be, that every one of us wants—a forty-inch TV maybe, but Hettie hasn't got that kind of money. So we throw on our jackets and troop out to the car, and there in the back is this sled, must be big enough for five people— four, anyway, and Becky can always scrunch up.

"Hettie, I swear, you're still a big kid," Dad says, while we haul it out, our grins saying our thank-yous.

"Can we try it out now?" Dara Lynn begs.

But Ma tells us the turkey's almost ready and folks'll be coming soon. "After dinner. And not till the dishes are done," she tells us.

So we just surround Aunt Hettie with a group hug

and move her inside. All I can think about is how much fun David Howard and me are going to have on that sled over Christmas vacation.

We got twelve people there at our table—the dining room table Ma inherited from her mother, Grandma Slater. It's got two extension boards for it, so when it's opened up as long as it will go, it stretches all the way into our living room.

Just after everyone gets here, it's awkward for a while, standing around the potbellied stove with cups of cider in our hands. Dad does the introductions, and when he gets to Judd and the preacher, I realize it's the first time they come face-to-face, yet one of 'em been preaching against the other, and that one cussing him out.

But once we sit down at the table, it's not so bad. There's a decorated name card at each place. I'm at one end with Dad; Ma and Becky are at the other, and then we got four more people on either side.

Of course, Pastor Dawes is asked to give the prayer. I'm hoping it's not one of his five-minute variety, 'cause we got sweet potatoes and turkey and dressing and green beans cooked with bacon waiting, all of it steaming hot. Preacher must be hungry too, 'cause he keeps it short. He don't mention sin or blasphemy, but he ends his prayer with, "Bless us as we partake of your bounty, for we know your love shines down wherever two or more believers are gathered in your name. Amen."

"Now, please, everyone just help yourself to whatever's closest to you and pass it around the table," Ma says. "Pastor, if you'll start the potatoes . . ."

"Call me Jacob," the preacher says, so Jacob it is. Wonder if his closest friends call him Jake. I could no more call him Jacob than I could stick my hand in the stove, but of course he means grown-ups, not kids.

Dara Lynn and Ruthie are sitting side by side, whispering and giggling through the meal. Rachel's beside her ma, but we grin at each other when I drop a little blob of sweet potatoes in the dish of green beans and try to dig it out. She's wearing a white sweater, and Ruthie's in a red one. Maybe it'd be easier to think of the preacher as "Jacob" if he had a red-and-white tie 'stead of the blue-and-black one he's got around his neck.

Doc Murphy asks Aunt Hettie where she was raised, and she tells him how she and Dad grew up in Ripley with their brothers, but two of those brothers moved out of state. "I can't ever imagine myself living in a place where I don't look out and see hills around me," she says. Now, she tells Doc, she works in a bank, but she can see hills on her way home.

"Was there ever a holdup at your bank?" asks Dara Lynn. If anyone can think of an inappropriate question to ask at the Christmas table, it's Dara Lynn. Couple weeks ago, she waits till we're eating dessert and tells how the school bus run over a possum that morning. She saw it. And when the bus was going home that afternoon, the insides of that possum was still out there on the road. Try to imagine *that* while you eat your cherry pie!

But it don't bother Aunt Hettie. "Not while I was working there," she says. "Though I saw a man come in with a ski mask on once and I hid under the counter, but he'd just forgot to pull it up off his face before he came in to make a deposit."

We laugh about that.

I manage to get some dark meat when the turkey comes to me, and almost wish we'd stop all the food making the rounds so I could take a bite of something.

Then Dara Lynn's question about bank robbers reminds Doc Murphy of the time a man come to his house at night and wants him to take a bullet out of his arm. Doc knows better than to ask how it come to be there. But all the while he's working on the man's arm, man gets so talkative he starts saying where he was going and where he was coming from, and later the police are able to track him down and arrest him for homicide.

But then the conversation goes back to Christmas again, and Mrs. Dawes tells us how her ma—the grandmother who's got the flu—used to make marshmallow fudge on Christmas Eve, and now she makes it with her girls.

"Do you have any?" Becky asks right off.

And everyone smiles when Mrs. Dawes answers that as a matter of fact, she does. "Rachel and Ruthie helped me make some yesterday, and I've brought it along to go with our dessert," she says. Becky and Dara Lynn both cheer.

I realize that Shiloh's not got his muzzle on my thigh, trying to look pitiful so I'll slip a bite his way. How come that dog's being so quiet? I wonder. My eyes travel around the table. Then I notice that Doc Murphy has his fork in his right hand, but his left hand is down at his side. And sure enough, every once in a while, I see a bite of turkey go from his right hand to his left, and if the room is real quiet that second, I hear the soft thump of a tail hit the floor.

"Where did you grow up, Jacob?" asks Dad. "Any marshmallow fudge in your background?"

"I'm afraid not," says the preacher. He picks up his napkin, wipes his mouth. "We did have a special dinner on the twenty-fifth, I remember, but Christmas was a time for reflection, not celebration."

Dara Lynn stops eating and studies him a minute. "Didn't you never have any fun?"

That seems to stop the preacher cold. "Well . . . I'm sure my brother and I climbed trees and played in the meadow. Must have, because we had a lot of trees. . . ." Preacher pauses. "But you see, my father believed that the whole point of being a child was to grow up, and of course, the whole point of growing up is to grow in God's grace so you can enter the kingdom of heaven."

"*Dying*, you mean?" says Dara Lynn. "The whole point of living is dying?"

Wished I'd said that. For once I really admired my sister.

"To become a credit to the Heavenly Father, and"— Pastor Dawes shakes his head, ever so slight—"I'm afraid my own father felt I never measured up, and often told me so."

Rachel steals a quick glance at him, then turns away again.

"Seems we have that in common, Jacob," Judd says,

first time he's said much of anything since the meal started. And when the preacher looks over at him, Judd says, "My dad let me know every day of my life that I didn't measure up, and to get his point across he took the belt to me."

There's a hush around the table.

Finally the preacher says, "Guess a parent does what he thinks is right. 'Spare the rod and spoil the child,' the good book says. But . . . I don't know. . . ."

"You think a child ever figures it's right?" says Judd. "You got a parent doing that way with a kid . . . saying those kinds of things to his boy . . . Don't come across as anything but pure meanness."

"The worst part is, if children don't know any different, they pass it along," says Doc Murphy.

The whole conversation's taken such a serious tone all of a sudden, hardly anybody can stop it. Not sure they should. I don't see that there's any foot nudging under the table.

And then Dad says, "But the *good* part is, their meanness can end with you. Don't have to let it go one more day."

"That would be a wonderful thing," says Mrs. Dawes.

Ma says, "The girls and I made some special cookies,

when everyone is ready. But please help yourselves to seconds and thirds."

"Let's get everything going around one more time," says Dad. "Doc, would you pass that dressing down my way?"

Hands start moving again, and there's chatter here and there. But at some point in the meal, just when I think maybe folks took Dad's words to heart, I hear the preacher say, "Rachel, you've got cranberry sauce on your new sweater."

I see the color rise in Rachel's cheeks, just like they did that first day of school on the bus. She stares down at her sweater, not knowing quite what to do. The spot is about the size of a pea. Ma fumbles around for a napkin, and then Becky leans forward and tells the preacher, "But the whole *rest* of her sweater is clean!"

Now we really are speechless, 'cause not a one of us could have thought of saying anything that perfect.

The preacher studies Becky a moment, then turns back to Rachel and says, "That's right. It's only a tiny spot. And Rachel, you and your sister look lovely in your new sweaters."

The girls are so shocked they stare at their father, and Ma adds, "Indeed they do! Now if everyone is through, you can pass your plates down to me and we'll think about dessert."

We pass our plates to the end of the table, where Mrs. Dawes is helping Ma scrape them off. Ma has mince and pumpkin pies to go along with her cookies and the fudge from the Daweses. I take a huge slab of fudge first, and boy is it good, but my mind's on the big sled Aunt Hettie brought us. I see that stack of dishes on the counter, though, and know that none of us are going sledding till those are clean and put away.

Then the grown-ups get to talking again, which tells me it's going to be a long time before that kitchen's cleaned up. I look around the table and notice that the preacher's got such a wistful look on his face, I turn to see where he's staring. I find that Becky has slid down from her chair and climbed up on Dad's lap, the way she'll do sometimes when she's tired of eating but don't want to miss out on grown-ups' conversation. She's snuggled down in the crook of his arm, twisting a lock of hair with one finger. Dad's eating his mince pie with his other hand and having a conversation with Judd about the little trailer he's got coming in January.

I look back at the preacher and see that his eyes are wet. Those are tears for sure—just enough to make his eyes watery. So I turn away and don't look back. It's a moment so personal he gets it all to himself.

With twelve people helping, those dishes are washed and dried and put away like nobody's business. The turkey's cut up and divided in little packets to go home with everybody for sandwiches the next day, and the minute the last cupboard door is closed, Dara Lynn sings out, "Sled time!"

I see the preacher look at his watch and can tell he wants to go home. We've had another inch or two of snow during dinner, but then it tapered off, and the roads shouldn't be too bad. I expect he'll say something about how he's got a sick person he's got to visit, but since he'd already set the day aside to take his family to their grandma's, he can't hardly expect anyone to take that seriously.

Since the Daweses hadn't known we were going sledding, though, the next five minutes is spent fishing more boots out of the closet, more caps and scarves and mittens. And when us five kids look like we're headed for Alaska and Dad's got on his work boots, we find a rope to put on the new sled and go out to the long hill behind the house.

Rachel and Ruthie hold back, wanting us to go first, see how it's done, so Dad tramps up the hill, Dara Lynn and Becky and me following behind. I want to go down all alone, so I volunteer to push them off. Dad sits down at the back of the sled, Dara Lynn in front of him, Becky in front of her, and then Dad stretches his long legs out so his feet are on the steering bar in front.

"Ready?" he asks. The girls lean back, Dara Lynn against Dad, Becky against her. I give them the hardest push I can manage, and the sled whizzes down that hill, the girls screamin' their heads off.

Dad knows where the stump of the old locust tree is buried in the snow, and he steers away from it, but the minute he gets to the bottom, he turns too quick to stop the sled and they all fall off, laughing and hooting.

I'm next. Take a running start to do a belly flop. Don't do much better than Dad when I get to the bottom, but man, that sled goes fast. Shiloh's running up and down the hill, following every sled trip to the bottom and back up again.

Now Ruthie's dancing up and down, pulling at Rachel's hand. "C'mon," I say. "Sled holds four," so Dara Lynn goes up with us. This time I'm the one in back with my feet on the steering bar, Rachel against me, Dara Lynn against her, and Ruthie in front. Dara Lynn and Ruthie are already screaming, and we haven't even took off yet.

I dig my fists in the snow to tip us forward, and then we shoot off. Got my hands holding tight to the sled on both sides, the girls holding on to each other, and I got to say, I make a perfect half circle when we get to the bottom.

Then Aunt Hettie says she's got to start back to Clarksburg pretty soon before the snow gets any deeper on the roads, but she's not going till she gets a chance on that sled herself. We all of us cheer as she lies down on her stomach and I give her a push. Gets halfway down—don't know what she hits—but she falls off the sled and it goes on without her, and she is lying there on her back in the snow, laughing like a kid. Shiloh goes over and licks her face, and she laughs some more.

"Hettie, you sound just like you did at thirteen," Dad says, going up the hill and helping her to her feet.

"Wanted to do that ever since I can remember," she said. "You boys always hogged our sled for yourselves, and it's about time I got a turn!"

"Well, take another," Dad says, and she does. Then we're all of us telling Judd to try it out.

So he climbs to the top of our hill, and we figure he'll take the same path the rest of us have taken. But he must have decided to carve out his own sled tracks there on the hill, 'cause he weaves first to one side, then the other, and even though Dad shouts a warning, he's heading right for where we know that tree stump is buried.

And suddenly Judd Norman Travers is airborne, that sled going up the slant side of the stump, and in that split second I see a look on his face that must have been his look when he was just a kid. And then he is down on the slope again, still holding on, and he gives this loud "Ye-haw!" that makes us laugh and clap, and when he gets off at the bottom, he's grinning wider than I can ever remember.

"Judd, I should've warned you about that stump," says Dad.

He shakes his head. "Best ride I ever had," he says. "Next time I try it, I'll have my dog with me," and we laugh some more.

Becky wants another ride, and then there's just a girls' ride, and I decide that my extra Christmas gift to Dara Lynn will be to hand the sled over to her each time she wants a ride. Finally the Daweses say it's time to go home.

"One more!" Ruthie pleads, and grabs for Dad's hand. "Take us up one more time!" she begs.

It's embarrassing there for a moment, her grabbing Dad's hand. He don't want it to look like Ruthie chooses him over her own dad, but don't know how to turn her down, neither.

And then we hear Jacob say, "I'll take you girls, but I need a pair of boots."

The girls can't believe it. *I* can't believe it. Can't take our eyes off their dad, and finally Ruthie's face breaks into the widest smile. I hear Dad say, "I got an old pair of galoshes, Jacob. I don't know your size, but they'd probably fit over most anybody's shoes."

And before you know it, the preacher's on his way up the hill, the galoshes making a gloppy sound on his feet. He's got one of Dad's caps on his head, one of Dad's scarves around his neck, and I go along to give them a push. He sits down at the back of the sled, and for a minute, I don't think Rachel's going to sit in front of him. But finally she does, then Ruthie.

"Ready?" I say. I see the preacher lean forward to grasp the sides of the sled, his chin next to Rachel's shoulder. She leans back against him just a little, Ruthie against her, and I give 'em a push, then follow them down the hill on my feet, Shiloh leaping along beside them through the snow.

I tell you, I can even hear the preacher give a shout, and when they turn at the bottom, Rachel snuggled back against her dad, their cheeks are apple red and they're all three of them smiling. When Ruthie begs to do it again, her father tells her, "Okay, one more time, and then we need to go."

I know that a single afternoon don't change a lifetime of preaching against sin. It don't change a lifetime of looking for faults instead of goodness, feeling fear instead of love. And it don't make Judd the kind of man you can trust 100 percent. But like Dad says, it could be a start.

Everyone goes home by four o'clock. Aunt Hettie's already on her way back to Clarksburg. We say Merry Christmas to the Daweses and Doc Murphy, and Judd heads down to his friend in Middlebourne to see his dog, take him some of that leftover turkey.

Then our family has the sled to ourselves. Even Ma bundles up and takes a few rides. We're on that hill a half hour more, but when the wind picks up, turning colder and raw, we pack it in for the night and go inside to warm up by the stove.

As we're taking off our boots, I hear Ma say to Dad, "Judith told me something interesting as we were watching the kids play. First she said she'd like to go to that parenting class with me, and then she said that Doc Murphy had suggested a counselor in Sistersville that he thought would be good for her and Jacob."

"Really!" says Dad.

"And she also said she's made an appointment, and she's going whether he goes or not," Ma tells him.

"Well, that's a step in the right direction," says Dad. "I don't know . . . Somehow, I think he might go along."

I don't say a word. Can't stop smiling.

When Judd comes back around eight, though, he discovers a big old branch has blown down on the tent, and new snow has got his sleeping bag wet.

Wind is fierce now, and after Dad takes a look at the situation, he says, "Judd, it's Christmas, and you're not sleeping out there tonight. We'll get to that tomorrow. Come on in here where it's warm."

And for once Judd agrees. Ma makes turkey sandwiches and a salad, and after supper we sit around the living room—turn out all the lights except the ones on the tree. Dara Lynn shows off how she's learned to play "Jingle Bells"—her version of it, anyway—on the harmonica Santa left in her stocking. If you ask me, Santa should've had better sense, but she loses interest in it as soon as she sees Becky trying to find something of Judd's to look at under her microscope. He offers a thread from his jeans or a hair, but she's already seen some of those.

"Tell you what," he says. "I got a callus on my hand

from chopping wood. You can have a piece of that." He pulls out his pocketknife, and Becky's fascinated as he peels off a thin piece of the thick skin.

"Gross!" says Dara Lynn, but she puts it between two glass slides and hands it to her sister. Becky slips the slide in place and turns on the little light. Then she bends low over the microscope and fixes her eye in the right place.

"Wow!" she cries. And moves over to give Dara Lynn a look.

Dara Lynn takes her place at the microscope.

Judd starts to grin. "What'd you find? No bugs, I hope."

"You're made up of all these teeny tiny pieces," says Dara Lynn.

"Yeah, I get to dancing too hard, I'm like to fall apart," Judd tells her. And when Becky don't smile, he says, "Just joking, sweetheart."

When it's time for bed, and the girls have gone off to put on their pajamas, I tell Judd he can have the couch tonight, but he says he can sleep just as well in a recliner. So while Ma brings out the pillows and blankets, I put the leash on Shiloh and take him out to do his business before we settle down for the night.

Don't have my boots on, so I stay on the bottom step

and let Shiloh nose around in the snow. Air is crisp as a cracker, sky so bright I can see stars I never knowed was up there before. Feel like I'm standing by a fairy-tale house, those icicle lights behind me. Dad says we get to keep them up till New Year's Day. Neighbors like 'em too.

When I go back in, Dad's turning out the light in the kitchen, and I thank him again for the desk lamp/radio he and Ma gave me. "It's really cool," I tell him.

He gives me a one-arm hug. "Now all you need is a room," he says. "Won't be long. We're working on it. G'night, Judd."

"Have yourself a good one," Judd says in reply.

He settles himself in the recliner, brings up the footrest so he can lean way back. I go to the bathroom and put on my pajamas. When I come out, I turn off the Christmas tree lights and crawl under my blanket there on the couch. The living room's dark except for the glow of our icicle lights coming in the windows, and a small square of yellow/orange from our potbellied stove.

Radio's still playing softly in the corner. Ma had it on all day so we'd have music during company dinner, and we like every little bit of Christmas we can get. Each one of us has got a favorite carol. Mine is "We Three Kings," 'cause you can hear someone using wood blocks to sound like camels' hoofs. Dara Lynn likes "O Holy

Night" just to see if the soprano can hit the high note without it wiggling.

Ma slips into the room and turns the radio off.

"Time for sleep," she whispers.

So I listen to the concert I got right here—the fire hissing and spitting; Judd Travers snoring in and out, in and out; and Shiloh's wheezy little breaths. And I figure this is about all the music I need.

———

A READING GROUP GUIDE TO

A  Christmas

Discussion Questions

1. The people who live in Friendly neither like nor approve of Judd Travers, even though he is trying to change. How does Judd prove to the townspeople that he has changed?

2. Judd, Marty, and Rachel have all been influenced by their parents. How has the parental influence felt by each character shaped that character's life and personality?

3. Dara Lynn thinks Ruthie is exaggerating when she talks about her father and the punishment he administers. Do you agree? How is exaggerating different from lying?

4. How do Marty's feelings change when Judd tells Marty about his past?

5. What are David's and Marty's reactions when they find Rachel locked in the shed? How do they respond? How does their perception of Rachel change as a result of the incident?

6. What do Marty's parents think about Pastor Dawes's Sunday messages? What do they learn about the pastor's life as a result of the sermons?

7. Why are Marty's parents concerned about Rachel and Ruthie? What occurs to lead Marty's parents to conclude that the girls are being abused by their dad?

8. Who are the people Marty trusts to answer his *why* questions? How does Marty become more wise, as a result of the people in his life and the answers he receives from them?

9. Why does Marty put his life in danger to save Judd's dogs? Why does Marty want to tell his parents? How do Marty's parents react to his confession?

10. Why are the people of Friendly convinced that Judd started the fire even after the investigation proves he is innocent? How does Judd react to their rudeness?

11. Why does Rachel run away? What does Judd do and say to help restore her to her family?

12. What parenting advice do Marty's parents give to the pastor and his wife? How does their advice help the pastor become a more loving father?

13. How does Doc Murphy encourage Marty's dream of becoming a vet? How does Dr. Collins encourage Marty's dream?

14. What is ironic about the way people judge Judd and the preacher? Of the two, who is the kinder person? What evidence in the novel supports your choice?

15. What does Marty learn about people and life as a result of the biography and autobiography assignment Mr. Kelly gives his students?

16. When Marty's dad talks to Judd about the preacher coming to Christmas dinner, Marty says, "Talk about smooth." What does Marty mean? How does his dad convince Judd to come for dinner?

17. When the preacher sees Becky climb into her dad's lap, why does he cry? How is this the beginning of change in the way the preacher treats his daughters?

Turn the page for a peek at the book
that started it all, *Shiloh*.

The day Shiloh come, we're having us a big Sunday dinner. Dara Lynn's dipping bread in her glass of cold tea, the way she likes, and Becky pushes her beans up over the edge of her plate in her rush to get 'em down.

Ma gives us her scolding look. "Just once in my life," she says, "I'd like to see a bite of food go direct from the dish into somebody's mouth without a detour of any kind."

She's looking at me when she says it, though. It isn't that I don't like fried rabbit. Like it fine. I just don't want to bite down on buckshot, is all, and I'm checking each piece.

"I looked that rabbit over good, Marty, and you won't find any buckshot in that thigh," Dad says, buttering his bread. "I shot him in the neck."

Somehow I wish he hadn't said that. I push the meat from one side of my plate to the other, through the sweet potatoes and back again.

"Did it die right off?" I ask, knowing I can't eat at all unless it had.

"Soon enough."

"You shoot its head clean off?" Dara Lynn asks. She's like that.

Dad chews real slow before he answers. "Not quite," he says, and goes on eating.

Which is when I leave the table.

The best thing about Sundays is we eat our big meal at noon. Once you get your belly full, you can walk all over West Virginia before you're hungry again. Any other day, you start out after dinner, you've got to come back when it's dark.

I take the .22 rifle Dad had given me in March on my eleventh birthday and set out up the road to see what I can shoot. Like to find me an apple hanging way out on a branch, see if I can bring it down. Line up a few cans on a rail fence and shoot 'em off. Never shoot at anything moving, though. Never had the slightest wish.

We live high up in the hills above Friendly, but hardly anybody knows where that is. Friendly's near Sistersville, which is halfway between Wheeling and Parkersburg. Used to be, my daddy told me, Sistersville was one of the best places you could live in the whole state. You ask *me* the best place to live, I'd say right where we are, a little four-room house with hills on three sides.

Afternoon is my second-best time to go up in the hills, though; morning's the best, especially in summer. Early, *early* morning. On one morning I saw three kinds of animals, not counting cats, dogs, frogs, cows, and horses. Saw a groundhog, saw a doe with two fawns, and saw a gray fox with a reddish head. Bet his daddy was a gray fox and his ma a red one.

My favorite place to walk is just across this rattly bridge where the road curves by the old Shiloh school-house and follows the river. River to one side, trees the other—sometimes a house or two.

And this particular afternoon, I'm about halfway up the road along the river when I see something out of the corner of my eye. Something moves. I look, and about fifteen yards off, there's this shorthaired dog—white with brown and black spots—not making any kind of noise, just slinking along with his head down, watching me, tail between his legs like he's hardly got the right to breathe. A beagle, maybe a year or two old.

I stop and the dog stops. Look like he's been caught

doing something awful, when I can tell all he really wants is to follow along beside me.

"Here boy," I say, slapping my thigh.

Dog goes down on his stomach, groveling about in the grass. I laugh and start over toward him. He's got an old worn-out collar on, probably older than he is. Bet it belonged to another dog before him. "C'mon, boy," I say, putting out my hand.

The dog gets up and backs off. He don't even whimper, like he's lost his bark.

Something really hurts inside you when you see a dog cringe like that. You know somebody's been kicking at him. Beating on him, maybe.

"It's okay, boy," I say, coming a little closer, but still he backs off.

So I just take my gun and follow the river. Every so often I look over my shoulder and there he is, the beagle. I stop; he stops. I can see his ribs—not real bad—but he isn't plumped out or anything.

There's a broken branch hanging from a limb out over the water, and I'm wondering if I can bring it down with one shot. I raise my gun, and then I think how the sound might scare the dog off. I decide I don't want to shoot my gun much that day.

It's a slow river. You walk beside it, you figure it's not

even moving. If you stop, though, you can see leaves and things going along. Now and then a fish jumps—big fish. Bass, I think. Dog's still trailing me, tail tucked in. Funny how he don't make a sound.

Finally I sit on a log, put my gun at my feet, and wait. Back down the road, the dog sits, too. Sits right in the middle of it, head on his paws.

"Here, boy!" I say again, and pat my knee.

He wiggles just a little, but he don't come.

Maybe it's a she-dog.

"Here, girl!" I say. Dog still don't come.

I decide to wait the dog out, but after three or four minutes on the log, it gets boring and I start off again. So does the beagle.

Don't know where you'd end up if you followed the river all the way. Heard somebody say it curves about, comes back on itself, but if it didn't and I got home after dark, I'd get a good whopping. So I always go as far as the ford, where the river spills across the path, and then I head back.

When I turn around and the dog sees me coming, he goes off into the woods. I figure that's the last I'll see of the beagle, and I get halfway down the road again before I look back. There he is. I stop. He stops. I go. He goes.

And then, hardly thinking on it, I whistle.

It's like pressing a magic button. The beagle comes barreling toward me, legs going lickety-split, long ears flopping, tail sticking up like a flagpole. This time, when I put out my hand, he licks all my fingers and jumps up against my leg, making little yelps in his throat. He can't get enough of me, like I'd been saying no all along and now I'd said yes, he could come. It's a he-dog, like I'd thought.

"Hey, boy! You're really somethin' now, ain't you?" I'm laughing as the beagle makes circles around me. I squat down and the dog licks my face, my neck. Where'd he learn to come if you whistled, to hang back if you didn't?

I'm so busy watching the dog I don't even notice it's started to rain. Don't bother me. Don't bother the dog, neither. I'm looking for the place I first saw him. Does he live here? I wonder. Or the house on up the road? Each place we pass I figure he'll stop—somebody come out and dog don't stop. Keeps coming even after we get to the old Shiloh schoolhouse. Even starts across the bridge, tail going like a propeller. He licks my hand every so often to make sure I'm still there—mouth open like he's smiling. He *is* smiling.

Once he follows me across the bridge, though, and on past the gristmill, I start to worry. Looks like he's fixing to follow me all the way to our house. I'm in trouble enough coming home with my clothes wet. My ma's mama died of pneumonia, and we don't ever get the chance to forget it. And now I got a dog with me, and we were never allowed to have pets.

If you can't afford to feed 'em and take 'em to the vet when they're sick, you've no right taking 'em in, Ma says, which is true enough.

I don't say a word to the beagle the rest of the way home, hoping he'll turn at some point and go back. The dog keeps coming.

I get to the front stoop and say, "Go home, boy." And then I feel my heart squeeze up the way he stops smiling, sticks his tail between his legs again, and slinks off. He goes as far as the sycamore tree, lies down in the wet grass, head on his paws.

"Whose dog is that?" Ma asks when I come in.

I shrug. "Just followed me, is all."

"Where'd it pick up with you?" Dad asks.

"Up in Shiloh, across the bridge," I say.

"On the road by the river? Bet that's Judd Travers's beagle," says Dad. "He got himself another hunting dog a few weeks back."

"Judd got him a hunting dog, how come he don't treat him right?" I ask.

"How you know he don't?"

"Way the dog acts. Scared to pee, almost," I say.

Ma gives me a look.

"Don't seem to me he's got any marks on him," Dad says, studying him from our window.

Don't have to mark a dog to hurt him, I'm thinking.

"Just don't pay him any attention and he'll go away," Dad says.

"And get out of those wet clothes," Ma tells me. "You want to follow your grandma Slater to the grave?"

I change clothes, then sit down and turn on the TV, which only has two channels. On Sunday afternoon, it's preaching and baseball. I watch baseball for an hour. Then I get up and sneak to the window. Ma knows what I'm about.

"That Shiloh dog still out there?" she asks.

I nod. He's looking at me. He sees me there at the window and his tail starts to thump. I name him Shiloh.

Did you LOVE reading this book?

Visit the Whyville...

EVERY GIRL SHOULD HAVE A FRIEND LIKE ALICE.